The Price
of Loyalty

The Price of Loyalty

Mike Castan

Holiday House / New York

Library of Congress Cataloging-in-Publication Data

Castan, Mike.

   The price of loyalty / by Mike Castan. — 1st ed.

    p. cm.

   Summary: Mexican American middle-schooler Manny finds himself caught between going along with his friends who are set on forming a gang and cutting his ties to them and following his own inclination to stay out of trouble.

   ISBN 978-0-8234-2268-5 (hardcover)

   [1. Gangs—Fiction. 2. Interpersonal relations—Fiction. 3. Conduct of life—Fiction. 4. Mexican Americans—Fiction. 5. Middle schools—Fiction. 6. Schools—Fiction. 7. Los Angeles (Calif.)—Fiction.] I. Title.

PZ7.C268586Pr 2011

[Fic]—dc22

2010024065

Dedicated to Amazing Grace

The Price of Loyalty

Chapter 1

RAIN HARDLY EVER CAME TO Orbe Nuevo. So when it finally did rain, it'd seem like a once-in-a-lifetime event. Just about every time rain would come, my abuela would yell from across the house, "Manny! Look outside. It's raining! It's raining!" The rain never lasted that long, maybe forty-five minutes. After it stopped my abuela would go outside and stand on the sidewalk, so she could chit-chat with the other abuelas. In Spanish they'd say how the rain made the air smell earthy and fresh, and how it was a nice break from the heat or wind. But then the hot or windy weather would return. And that would be all the rain Orbe Nuevo would have for what felt like a year.

What seemed the worst was when it rained and I was stuck in school all day. I always thought our school should give kids rain days when it rained, just so we could see what the rain looked like—the way some schools gave kids snow days when it snowed. If it was raining while I was at school, I would hear it falling on the roof and wish that I could run outside to feel it. But Orbe Nuevo Middle School had hazardous weather rules, which meant we couldn't have PE outside or go out in the rain. Instead I'd be stuck indoors all day.

Now being stuck inside Orbe Nuevo all day isn't all that bad, but it isn't like winning the World Cup either. My school is big, much bigger than elementary, where I'd gone for kindergarten through sixth grades. My first few weeks at middle school back in August, I got lost almost every day going to my classes. It didn't seem to matter, though. There were so many students coming and going that it could get pretty confusing for anybody. It had huge cement buildings with iron gates.

Those first weeks of school were right about the time that the gang was starting to come together. No whites. No blacks. Only Latinos could join the Conquistadors. It mostly started because Hernan, Cisco, and I were all friends from elementary school, ever since kindergarten. Hernan and Cisco were cousins, and they had some friends who went to other elementary schools in the area who wound up at Orbe Nuevo, too. When we all started eating lunch together at the same table, the other kids began calling us a gang.

Then one day at lunch, a girl at a nearby table shouted over to us, "Ah, you think you're all bad! What do you call yourselves?"

I had just been in social studies class where we learned about the Conquistadors, so I joked, "The Conquistadors!"

"Yeah, girl. So show some respect," Hernan added.

Everybody seemed to like the name, so it stuck.

Right about that time I noticed a change with how the other kids treated us. Some of it was because Hernan and Cisco both had brothers who grew up in the area. They had gone to the same schools as we did, too, but years before. Now they were in trouble a lot and some were even in prison. Because of the older homeboys' hard-core reputations, we got them, too. So the Conquistadors gang was born, and we were all members, just like that. Later on other kids would want to join, but it wasn't easy. Just getting into the Conquistadors took a lot of guts. If you stepped up without an invitation or a sponsor you could get whupped just for asking.

Next, Hernan got called into the principal's office for making a gang sign with his fingers in English class. When he told us the story later he was cool about it, but I knew Hernan, and I knew he had been scared. Walking home from school that afternoon, he hardly said anything. And when he did say something, it was, "From now on, nobody talks about the Conquistadors." From this, me and the other guys understood that the gang was still alive but we couldn't say anything about it.

That was okay by me. I was just relieved that I didn't get called into the principal's office, too. My abuela would have killed me. She'd always told me to stay away from trouble and troublemakers, because even if I didn't do anything, just the fact that I was near them could get me into trouble. I knew what she meant because I'd seen it happen. My mom and pop would've freaked out big time, too, if they'd found out I'd gotten busted and sent to the principal's office. Even though I only saw them every six months or so, I always heard my parents' voices in the back of my head, saying, "*¡No hagas las ondas!—Don't make waves!*"

As I soon discovered, it was hard to be in the Conquistadors but not make waves.

One thing I noticed early on was that some people took the Conquistadors more seriously than others. With Nando, Ferdinand, and me, it was just an act that we started to put on because kids expected it. But with Hernan and Cisco, it seemed like a new religion was being born. Just a few weeks after the kids started calling us the Conquistadors, Hernan and Cisco began to change. They didn't wear their usual clothes; it became nothing but white T-shirts and baggy jeans. And the changes didn't stop there.

Suddenly you couldn't be seen reading or doing homework. I had always gotten good grades. I liked to read; I'd always read above my level during Reading period. My favorite books were by Paul Zindel and S.E. Hinton, and I really liked this one story about a fisherman who was on a boat by himself, trying to reel in this big fish, by a guy named Hemingway. There was another book I liked that my sixth grade teacher had given me, about a poor family from Oklahoma who came out to California to find work. It was by a guy named Steinbeck. My sixth grade teacher had said I could read it over the summer and bring it back to her. It was so cool that I read it in four days and gave it back to her before the last day of school. The book reminded me of the stories that my parents told about coming to the United States, and how they had to hide, and creep, and pretend all the time just to stay here. And how *I* had to hide, and creep, and pretend all the time, just to do my homework.

The trouble started when Hernan got into a showdown with our math and science teacher. One day the teacher was collecting homework at the beginning of class. Hernan didn't have his. The teacher said he was going to call home because this was the second time in a week Hernan didn't have his work, and Hernan said, "Good. Go ahead, *pendejo!*" I had turned around in my seat to watch what was happening and had to shut my eyes and slap my forehead when I heard Hernan say the words. I knew I wouldn't see him in school for the rest of the week, that he'd be suspended because this would be his second referral in two weeks. More importantly, I knew Cisco wasn't going to turn in *his* homework because Hernan didn't turn in his, because he wanted to be seen as being down with his *vato*. And Cisco would be watching to see if I turned in mine, which meant I couldn't.

After the security guard escorted Hernan out of class with a referral, the teacher went back to collecting homework. When he got to Cisco's desk, Cisco shrugged and made a motion that he didn't have his work, even though I could see it sticking out of his notebook. But when the teacher got to my desk, he stopped for a second with a strange look on his face. As I shook my head to let him know I didn't have it, I knew what he was thinking. We'd been in school for two months and I hadn't missed turning in one assignment. My tests were all A's, too. He knew I had it. He stared at me without saying anything and then walked on.

From that day on, I made sure that I told the Conquistadors I had to use the bathroom or get a drink of water during pass period before class. Then I'd run around the building to get to class before the others so I could turn in my homework on the teacher's desk instead of waiting for him to collect it. After a couple of days of that, the teacher got a basket for homework and put it by the door.

The next change the Conquistadors made was with our haircuts. This happened after Hernan showed me a picture of his brother who was locked up. He was posing with a couple of his *vatos* standing around him. They were flashing signs with their fingers and they all had shaved heads. Hernan told me he was going to shave his head, and that I should, too, so we'd all look alike. I didn't think he was serious about it, yet the next Monday he walked right into homeroom with a cleanly-shaven head. Cisco had early detention for using profanity so I didn't see him until P.E. But when I finally ran into him, I wasn't too surprised to see that he had the same new haircut. I got an uncomfortable ache in my stomach as I realized that I'd have to shave my head, too, no matter what my abuela said.

My abuela wasn't my real abuela. My real abuelas were back in Mexico, and I could barely remember them. My American abuela was actually my baby-sitter; as I grew up I just called her abuela. Then my parents went back to Mexico. They decided I'd have a better chance at going to college some day if I stayed behind. So when my abuela offered to keep me while they went back home, they saw it as a lucky break. I didn't mind either, because my abuela let me watch TV or game when my homework was done, and she let me game all night long on the weekends. She never even checked my games to see if they were the right age for me. My mom and pop would never have let me get away with that.

The only problem I had with my American abuela was that she made me go to Mass every Sunday. Even though I believed in God, I got bored in church. There was one good side to it, though. My abuela liked to go to a church that was miles away from our neighborhood. That worked out fine for me because none of the guys would see me with my lame old Sunday clothes on. My abuela would make me get dressed all wimpy, with a tie and black shiny shoes. She wouldn't let me spike my hair with gel, either. I had to wash it clean and comb it. That was all going to change now, because I had to shave my head.

The Tuesday after Hernan and Cisco showed up with shaved heads, Nando and Bartolomeu came to school with theirs shaved, too. Nando was a member of the Conquistadors, but Bartolomeu was just a wannabe. He wasn't even jumped in yet, and he was already falling in line. My nerdy friend Nicky, who sat behind me in social studies, noticed enough to ask, "When are *you* getting your hair cut, Manny?" That was it. If even Nicky knew I had to do it, then I had to do it.

That night, after I told my abuela that I was going to the park to play soccer with the guys, I waited outside of Henrietta's parents' garage. Henrietta's pop worked at a tattoo parlor, but he also gave haircuts out of his garage for cheap. He knew how to draw really well, too, and gave cool tattoos for ten bucks a half hour. But only if you were cool—not to rat-kids who'd tell their parents where they got them.

As I sat on the curb waiting for him to get home from work, I wondered how I could hide the new haircut from my abuela. There'd be no way. She would just have to see my head and get upset. As the reality of the situation settled in, Henrietta's pop's truck turned around the corner and came creeping toward the house. He pulled into the driveway and came to a stop.

"¡Órale!" Henrietta's pop called as he got out of the truck.

"¡Órale!" I replied.

I could tell Henrietta's pop was a little drunk. Everybody knew the tattoo shop was where all the guys hung out to talk smack and drink beer, so by the time Henrietta's pop got home he'd be high as a kite.

He stepped out of his truck, clutching a pack of beer. After locking up, he waved for me to follow him.

Inside the garage, Henrietta's pop pointed to a barber chair. There was a cherry hot rod with the hood open on the other side of the garage. All over the walls were hand-drawn pictures of low-riders and *cholos*. He then turned on the stereo and popped in an oldies CD. An old lowrider song started playing on the stereo, and as he swayed to the music you could see he loved playing his oldies. On weekend nights, even two blocks away at my abuela's, I could hear the music of Thee Midniters and Brenton Wood playing from his garage.

"¿*Cuál quieres?*—Which one do you want?" he asked, mid-sway.

"*Numero uno*," I replied simply. He knew which one I meant. It was the cut all the *vatos* wanted. It was called a number one blade shave because all he needed on the razor was the number one blade guard.

Before cutting, Henrietta's pop cracked open a fresh beer and picked up his razor from a table next to the chair. He grabbed a sheet from the back of the chair, flung bits of hair off it, then wrapped it around me. He paused to drink half his beer, then began cutting. The razor was cold as it vibrated and buzzed off the first row of my hair. I feared what I would look like once the cut was done. Maybe my head would look too big. Or maybe it would look too pale. Behind the garage door I could hear Henrietta and her mom and baby sister in the kitchen. It sounded like they were cooking. After a while they opened the door and I got really embarrassed. Henrietta's baby sister ran out to give her pop a kiss, then ran back into the kitchen to play. Henrietta and her mom kept looking into the garage and smiling, which made me even more embarrassed. It bugged me the way girls would look sometimes, like they knew something about me that I didn't, like they knew I was going to look stupid with a shaved head.

When Henrietta's pop finished my haircut, he handed me a mirror. At first I didn't recognize the person looking back at me. Then it started to sink in that the guy was me. I was darker than the other guys so my scalp looked paler than my face. Hanging out in the sun for a while would fix that, I guessed. Henrietta's pop handed me a can of beer. I'd had some beer before at a party when my pop wasn't looking, but I'd never been given a can right in front of everybody. I wanted to look cool, so I took it. I handed him the five-dollar bill I'd brought for the haircut and he reached into his pocket and pulled out a wad of cash that looked about three inches thick. Carefully he slipped the five over the wad of bills and put it back into his pocket. Just then, Henrietta's mom looked out and saw the can of beer in my hand. She flipped out and started screaming at Henrietta's pop.

"*¡Tonto loco! Pendejo!* Don't give him *cerveza!*"

Unfazed, he started laughing.

Henriettas parents' fights were infamous. Three or four times the cops had come out to the house to break them up. A couple of times Henrietta's pop had been walked out to the cop's car with his hands cuffed behind his back. I made the decision to leave. Jumping up, I put the beer down, and took the sheet off.

"*Gracias,*" I said to Henrietta's pop, then gave a quick wave to the family in the kitchen.

It was dark outside when I got back on the street. I felt a chill on my scalp as I made my way toward my block; the air seemed to be coolly whizzing past my head. As I walked by the neighbors' houses, I wondered if any of them could see me with my new haircut. I wondered if they thought I was in a gang.

I was almost home when I ran into Hernan and Cisco. They said they'd just been at my abuela's house.

"We're going to Memorial Park to jump in Bartolomeu. Let's go!" Herman said, without breaking his stride.

I just followed. Hernan and Cisco were really moving; I had to take two steps for every one of theirs. Not wanting my abuela to see my haircut, I would've done anything at that point to avoid her.

Walking into the night, we went far past where the street-lights ran out. Memorial Park was way up on the northside of town. When we got there Ferdinand and Nando were already waiting for us by the swings. Ferdinand had a broken baseball bat, and Nando was pitching rocks to him.

"¡Órale!" Hernan shouted to the other guys when we got near.

"Hey, what's up?" they shouted back.

Bartolomeu hadn't got there yet, so we had to plan out what we were going to do.

"I say we just tag team him," Ferdinand said, hopping up to stand on the seat of the swing. Standing and swinging, he yelled out, "I say we just whup! Whup! Whup!"

The guys started laughing because Ferdinand was acting so lame.

"Hey, *pendejo*! Stop swinging," Hernan said, laughing.

After Ferdinand jumped off the swing, Hernan grew serious. Hunching over like in a football huddle, he directed, "Now here's what we're going to do. Two minutes straight we just beat on him. All of us at the same time. Just non-stop. He's supposed to stay on his feet. No groin. Everything else is fair."

As we all nodded in agreement, I wondered, How am I going to get out of this?

Chapter 2

THE ONLY LIGHT IN THE park came from the moon and some streetlights far off in the distance. If I had been in that park by myself I would've been scared. So I was glad the guys were there. I was just down over the fact that we were there to jump in Bartolomeu.

I'd known Bartolomeu since second grade. I went to his birthday parties. His mom always made tres leches cake. When we were little we had played on the same t-ball team. How many times was I going to have to do something like this? I couldn't say anything to Hernan, Ferdinand, Cisco, or Nando. They all seemed so excited; they were having fun with the whole Conquistadors thing. Maybe I could ask them to bend the rules because it was Bartolomeu and we'd all known him for such a long time. No, that would make me look weak, I reminded myself, and I kept smiling and laughing just to go along with the others. Maybe I could say that I was feeling sick and wanted to go home, but that would probably make me look even more chicken.

Bartolomeu wasn't late. He showed up right on time, at eight-fifteen. I could see him coming out of the darkness of the park with his white T-shirt on. He was strutting. Every few steps he would turn his head to the side and spit. He was ready for a fight. It then occurred to me that I had never been in a fight before.

Hernan took the lead as we stepped out of the sandbox and started walking toward Bartolomeu, five across. Bartolomeu didn't break his stride. We stopped a few feet apart.

"So you want to be down with us?" Hernan asked.

"Let's do it," Bartolomeu replied.

"Two minutes. You got to stay on your feet. No groin," Hernan said.

"Who's watching the time?"

My eyes darted around from wrist to wrist of all the Conquistadors. No one had a watch on. Before looking down to my own wrist, I asked God to please help me have it on. It was a miracle—my watch *was* on. There were so many mornings that I forgot to put it on, but right at that moment I had it. Still, I couldn't look too eager to be the timekeeper. I had to wait for the order from the guys.

"Sorry, Manny," Hernan said with regret. "You got to watch the time."

"Ah man! That's messed up," I replied with my lips, but thanked God in my heart.

"All right. Let's go," Bartolomeu answered back, clenching his fists.

And just like that, it was on. I didn't know what to do at first as I watched all the guys swarm Bartolomeu. For about five seconds I just watched, before remembering that I had to keep the time. Fists were flying everywhere. I guess Bartolomeu had decided

12

that he was going to be the first kid to actually be tougher than the gang he was getting jumped into, because he put up one crazy fight. He kept the four Conquistadors busy, shrugging off any belt he'd take and then coming back with a fury of fists. But the tide soon turned, and Bartolomeu couldn't hold off all the hits. He kept his hands up and tried to throw punches, but there was nothing behind them. As the two-minute mark approached, I could see that Bartolomeu was barely going to make it. The Conquistadors were thrashing him now, and I could see smears of blood all over Bartolomeu's face. He was whupped.

"Time—¡Alto!" I shouted out when the time was up.

Hernan let out a howl and dropped down to his knees in exhaustion. The others fell to the ground, too, on all fours. Then somewhere—I'm not sure where it started—I heard what sounded like sobbing. I was shocked, and wondered which Conquistador would let any of the other Conquistadors see him crying. Then I realized that it wasn't sobbing. It was laughing. Then another Conquistador began to chuckle, too, and then someone else. Soon we were all howling into the night.

Bartolomeu was now an official member of the Conquistadors, and everybody was happy—except me. What kept me from being happy along with the other guys was remembering that we were all going home now, and my abuela would see my haircut.

When I came through the front door, I could hear by the sound of the TV coming from the family room that my abuela was up. If I was lucky, I just might be able to sneak upstairs without her noticing.

"Manny! Is that you?" my abuela called out.

"Yeah, it's me," I replied, hopping onto the stairs without changing direction.

"Why are you so late? It's nine-thirty."

"I know. We were playing at the park. It was a tie score. We had to do penalty kicks."

"Dinner's on the counter."

"Not hungry."

"I made your favorite, *pozole* and tortillas."

"Not hungry. I got to finish my homework."

"I *have* to finish my homework," my abuela corrected.

"I'll be upstairs."

As I made my way up to my room, I wondered if it seemed odd to my abuela that she wasn't able to set eyes on me. Normally, if something was odd, she would be up to my room to find out what was going on. But if she didn't notice anything out of the ordinary, I wouldn't have to see her until the morning. If I was really lucky, there was a game show on TV. My abuela wouldn't stop watching a game show even if the house was on fire.

When I got to my room, I sat down at my desk to do homework. That way, if my abuela did come up to see what was going on, at least she would see me doing my work. I got my books out, but I couldn't concentrate. I started thinking about Bartolomeu and all that he went through just to be a member of the Conquistadors. All that, just for some made-up gang. My pop would think it was stupid, taking a beating for nothing, and with nobody paying you to do it, either. The way my pop would see it, it would be different if it was a prizefight for money, or you were fighting to get a job or something. But to take a beating like that just to be in a club, that was just plain *loco*.

I knew he was right. But it seemed like we were all swept up into something that had a life of its own. Even though I knew the Conquistadors were just a made-up gang, people believed it actually meant something. And because of that, the way people believed, it *did* mean something. I could see by the way Hernan and Cisco were getting respect at school that they were hooked.

Just then the doorknob turned. I didn't look up from my books. I kept pretending to study.

"You sure you're not hung—"

My abuela stopped mid-sentence. I could feel her staring at me. She didn't say anything for a long time.

"What happened to your hair?"

Finally I had to turn and look. When I did, I wished I hadn't. I could see the hurt in her eyes.

"One of the kids cut it. All the kids have a haircut like this."

"All the cholos have a haircut like that," my abuela corrected. She spoke to me in this soft and slow and hurt tone I'd never heard before. "Why do you want to look like that? That's not good, Manny. Now everybody will think you're in a gang. Are you in a gang, Manny?"

"No."

It hurt to lie to my abuela like that, but I wanted her to stop feeling sad.

The next morning I left for school real early, before my abuela got up, so I wouldn't run into her. As I walked to school, I felt miserable. How could I be so stupid? I should have just told the guys I wouldn't cut my hair, that I liked it long. I didn't think I could feel any worse that day. Then I got to school.

Things went pretty smooth through first and second period, but during the pass period between second and third, I walked into something I wish I hadn't. Right next to blacktop, I noticed a group of kids in a circle. Hernan was in the middle, with Cisco close by. I saw Hernan shouting something at Victor. I thought they were just clowning each other, you know, like making fun of each other's clothes. I wanted to hear what they were goofing on, but as I got closer, I realized that it wasn't clowning.

"How can you say you didn't know Nando was a Conquistador?" Hernan angrily asked. "You knew he was a Conquistador. Everybody knows he's a Conquistador! You don't rat on Conquistadors."

"That's messed up, man!" Victor replied. "I wasn't ratting on him. I'm not getting in trouble for something I didn't do."

"Then how'd the teacher find out Nando was trash-talking Deena then, huh? Huh?"

As I stood in the circle, I noticed Nando wasn't around. Standing next to Bartolomeu, I asked him what happened.

"Nando got sent to the principal's office 'cause Victor said he was trash-talking Deena in homeroom."

Hernan threw his index finger in Victor's face. "You a rat!"

"So whatcha' gonna' do about it?" Victor asked indifferently.

I turned around to see where the security guard was. She was looking the other way. When I turned back, all I saw was Hernan's fist hitting Victor right in the middle of his face. Victor instantly dropped to the ground holding his nose. He was breathing real heavy and started to spit out what looked like blood.

"Let's see you rat now, rat!" Cisco yelled at Victor.

Everyone turned around to see where the security guard was. She was still busy watching some other kids.

Hernan shouted to Victor, "Never snitch on the Conquistadors! You hear me, fool?"

Just then, the bell rang. I looked down at Victor on all fours on the ground and wanted to help him up, but I couldn't move. I knew I couldn't be seen helping him. He was done as far as the

Conquistadors were concerned. And if he was done, that meant I couldn't even talk to him anymore.

Kids started going to class; the circle broke up. Cisco and Hernan nudged me away. That's when I got real scared. This was going to guarantee us all a trip to the principal's office.

From that point on, the day moved in slow motion for me. We had English next, and I figured it would only be a matter of minutes before security came and got us all. Bartolomeu, Hernan, Cisco, and me would be escorted to the principal's office and sent home on suspension. My abuela would come to pick me up in the car and ignore me all the way home. Then she'd go inside the house and cry and do the sign of the cross over herself all night long like she did when her real son, Vasco, got into trouble, before he got sent to prison.

All during third period I couldn't concentrate in English. The teacher noticed and came by to check my work three or four times. Every time the phone rang or the door opened I just knew it was the principal or security looking for us. Third period finally ended and we made it to PE. I could hardly pay attention as the PE teacher made us do drills for our state fitness. He asked if I had a cold or something; I just shrugged and he left me alone. Then lunch came. Pizza was served, which was usually one of my favorites, but I could barely eat half a slice. I felt like I was swallowing rocks.

I didn't have science or math with Hernan, Cisco, and the other guys, and I wondered if they got busted while I was in class and my name hadn't come up yet. But I made it all the way through the bell at the end of sixth period, then out the door and all the way to the school gates. Hernan and Cisco were waiting for me.

As we walked home together, I asked Hernan and Cisco if anything had happened with the thing.

"Nah. He ain't gonna rat. He's too scared," Cisco said.

"I heard he told the PE teacher that he got hit with a soccer ball during pass period," Hernan added. "He even went to the nurse's office and told her that, too. We taught him not to rat."

"What if his mom and dad say something?" I asked.

"They won't," Hernan assuredly. "Hey, check this out."

Hernan kind of looked around with his eyes to see if anybody was watching. Carefully he took his denim jacket off his shoulder and showed me the inner lining. Tucked down each sleeve of the jacket were cans of spray paint, with a safety pin holding each sleeve closed so the cans wouldn't fall out.

"Hey, what's up with that?" I asked, not sure what he was going to do with the paint.

"You gotta sneak out tonight at one. We'll meet you right down by the gates to the wash."

"What are we going to do?"

"We got to mark our turf. We're gonna tag the wash," Hernan explained.

I swallowed hard before speaking. I wasn't sure how the guys were going to take what I was about to tell them.

"I can't do it. My abuela already thinks something's up. She doesn't sleep that deep. I'll get caught for sure."

Cisco jumped in. "Come on. You got to, man! It's Conquistadors' business. We all could get caught. Ain't no different for us."

Hernan added, "It's Friday. She's not going to check on you. Just leave your gamebox on. She's going to think you're gaming all night anyway."

We came to my street. As I stopped to turn down my block, I wanted to tell the guys that I couldn't make it. Nothing I could say could make them change their minds, but if I didn't go along, they would take it like I didn't want to be friends anymore. Eight years of friendship was hanging in the balance. I couldn't say no.

"All right. I'll be there," I said, looking them dead in the eye.

"Yeah! That's what I'm talking about. That's a Conquistador!" Cisco said with authority.

Hernan smiled. "All right, homeboy. Bring your best tag."

I nodded, turned around, and walked home.

Chapter 3

MY ABUELA IS A VERY clever old lady. She can sense when something is up. One time when I was little, I had taken a pack of gum from a convenience store without paying for it. I just took it off the display on the counter and put it in my pocket. The cashier didn't even notice. I didn't chew it or anything. I didn't tell anybody what I had done. But when I got home, my abuela knew.

"Manny, what did you do?"

I'd pretended not to know what she was talking about. I'd shrugged and sighed but finally I had to give in and tell her what I'd done. She made me take the gum back to the store and pay for it from out of my savings jar. The cashier didn't even want the money after I gave him the gum back, but my abuela made me give it to him. So how was I possibly going to sneak out of the house after midnight without her knowing?

The best thing I could think of to distract my abuela from finding out was to not think about sneaking out. I just wouldn't think about it until I went. She wouldn't be able to sense it or see it on my face because it wouldn't be on my mind. As soon as I got home from school I told her I was playing a new game and went straight to my room. I left the door open so she could see me, and I played. I played from four o'clock in the afternoon until seven-thirty when my abuela came to bring me dinner.

"Wow. This must be a good game," she said, putting a plate of dinner next to me on the floor.

"It's all right," I replied without looking up from the screen. "I'm just learning how to play this one. I keep getting killed on the first level."

"Ew, Manny. Can't you say something else beside that?" My abuela made the sign of the cross over herself. "Killed, ew!"

I smiled and thanked her for dinner.

Between bites of dinner I kept playing, until I remembered that I had to come up with a tag for the Conquistadors before I went out later.

A tag is supposed to be the sum of who you are in a just a few drawn lines. It can be a picture or a number or letters. Most of the Conquistadors already had one; you could see them on their notebooks and backpacks. Sometimes they'd carve them with a penknife onto the desks at school. Cisco got caught for doing it just a few weeks back. He tried to deny it, but our math teacher saw the same tag all over his notebook.

I took out a sheet of notebook paper and started to brainstorm. I started with my name and tried to make something work with that, but then I thought about how it might come back to me, like it did with Cisco. I couldn't think of any numbers that made any sense for me, so I started drawing symbols instead. I thought about how we were the Conquistadors, and how conquistadors wear helmets. So I made a helmet that looked all right, I settled on that and started gaming again.

I gamed straight until ten-thirty when I heard my abuela calling from down the hall.

"Manny. I'm going to bed. That's bad for your circulation. Get up and stretch sometime. Drink some water or juice, too. No soda."

"Okay," I called back to her. "I will."

That was good, I thought. She actually gave me an excuse to get up and move around. But that wasn't the same as letting me leave the house after midnight. I kept gaming and watching the clock. Before I knew it, it was twelve-fifteen. I was sure that I was going to get into big trouble, but I had to do it. I'd told the guys I would.

I got up from gaming and cautiously stepped to my bedroom door. I pulled the door open a little bit to look down the hall. I saw a sliver of light underneath my abuela's door, not a lot so I figured it must've been the TV. Sometimes she slept with the TV on. Closing the door, I looked around my room for a white T-shirt. I didn't know why, but that's what all the Conquistadors wore.

Finally finding a T-shirt, I pulled it on, then looked out my window. It was fall, and the winds were blowing. I sighed as I thought about going outside in the cold wind. I don't care what the guys think, I decided, I'm wearing something over my shirt. I pulled out a plaid wool shirt that belonged to my abuela's son, Vasco, and put it on. "*Pendejo,*" I whispered under my breath as I realized I was about to leave without putting on shoes. I tied my Chuck T's and quietly left the room. I left my gamebox on, like Hernan suggested.

I snuck down the stairs, looking up once to see if my abuela was stirring. Then I started off down the street, silently closing the door behind me.

It was late Friday night so there were still a lot of cars driving around the neighborhood. I could hear Henrietta's pop's oldies music coming from their house a couple blocks away. And I could hear Mariachi music playing at a couple of other houses. There were loud voices and laughter from a few garages and backyards, so there must have been some partying going on. It felt kind of fun to be out walking the streets after midnight. I felt a little like I was a high schooler or something. What if the cops stop me? I wondered. I'll just tell them I was gaming at a friend's house and now I'm going home.

The wash was about a half mile away from my house. It was about the same distance away for the other guys, too. When we were little, a few years back, we'd go there in the summer to play. Sometimes there'd be small pools of water there where we could find pollywogs and tiny frogs. We'd catch them, put them in empty milk cartons, and take them home. Sometimes they would live for a couple of days, but mostly they would die before we got home with them. A couple of times Hernan, Cisco, and I tried to walk north up the wash all the way to the Creek. We'd only make it a mile or so before getting tired and turning back. There were a couple bridges on the way up North and that's where everybody liked to put their tags. There was some really nice graffiti art, too. Guys from our neighborhood had been going there for years to practice their tags, and now it was our turn.

It didn't take me long to get to the gates of the wash. The guys were waiting for me. Hernan and Cisco had already climbed over the fence and were throwing rocks down the embankment. Nando, Bartolomeu, and Ferdinand were waiting outside the gates as lookouts.

"Whassup, Manny?" Nando called out as he saw me coming down the street.

The guys were all shivering and had their hands dug in their pockets. I was glad I had brought my overshirt.

"Hey guys! What's up?" I yelled back.

When they saw me coming, Nando, Bartolomeu and Ferdinand started to climb the fence. We'd been climbing the fences since we were little, but now, as I looked on from a distance, I saw how risky the climb really was. The fences were about twelve feet high and had three layers of barbed wire running along the tops. As I watched, Ferdinand tried to flip over the top like he'd done hundreds of times before, and one of his shoelaces got caught on the barbed wire.

"Guys! Guys! Hey guys! I'm stuck!" he yelled out.

Hernan and Cisco ran up the embankment and started laughing.

"Check him out!" Hernan pointed and laughed harder.

"It's not funny, man. Come on. I'm gonna fall!"

I started to climb the fence near Ferdinand. I couldn't help but laugh a little, too. He was hanging upside down with his shoe caught on the barbed wire and a few fingers locked into the chain link to support him.

When I got to where Ferdinand was, I started to pull his shoelace off the fence.

Still laughing, the guys yelled out, "Leave him up there, man!"

Ferdinand cleared the top of the fence and made his way down on the other side. I followed after him to reach the other guys, and then we set out. It wasn't too far to the bridge that we were going to tag, but it felt like it was because it was after midnight and we could all get into big trouble if anyone found out. The wash was a long dry riverbed that only flowed when a lot of rain came. It was rocky and dangerous at parts. It was also home to a lot of cats, rats, and coyotes. The coyotes would use the wash as their freeway to come down from the foothills and higher lands when food was scarce, or when there was a fire or flood. Sometimes kids would say they saw mountain lions or even bears down in the wash, but nobody really believed them.

And, of course, there were rattlesnakes. One time last summer, Hernan, Cisco, and I had heard what sounded like a rattlesnake behind some rocks, and we'd jammed away from there faster than jack rabbits. Wanting to be macho, Hernan went back. As Cisco and I looked on from a distance, he held up a plastic grocery bag that had been caught on a tumbleweed and was blowing in the wind.

"Hey! Chickens!" Hernan had called out. "Here's your rattlesnake! Looks like a diamondback!" He howled with laughter.

As we walked along now, stumbling over rocks and trash, I wondered if there might be a mountain lion or bear watching our every move. Then I remembered that no mountain lion or bear could be any scarier than the look my abuela was going to give me if she found out we were in the wash after midnight.

We could see that we were getting closer to the overpass. It looked huge and dark. Every now and then a car would drive over it, and then it would go dark again. It made me wonder how were we going to see what we were tagging.

"Hey," I called out. "Hey guys. How are we going to see?"

"Don't worry about it. I got it," Hernan replied. He pulled out a cigarette lighter from the jacket he had flung over his shoulder. Testing it, he started flicking the spark.

When we got under the overpass it was dark and spooky. Homeless people had left behind old sofas, and there were piles of trash. Alex dropped to his knees and started a fire with the trash. The small fire grew until our figures made huge shadows on the walls.

The walls of the overpass were covered with graffiti. There

were hundreds of tags and pictures and four-letter words. There was some nice art there, too. As I looked at the walls, I noticed the familiar style of Henrietta's pop's art. He must have done the pictures years before, when he was our age. I wondered where we were going to put our tags, because there wasn't any room.

Hernan divvied up the cans of spray paint and said, "Just pick out a spot."

"Where?" I replied.

"Anywhere."

Hernan found where his brothers had put their tags years earlier, so he started putting his up there, too. Cisco did the same thing when he found his brothers' tags. Bartolomeu and Nando found patches of white on a mural and started working on theirs. Ferdinand and I looked on, still wondering where to put ours. There was a small blank patch on the wall. So I climbed over some brush to put my tag there.

I shook the spray paint can a few times to get it going and all of sudden I heard a siren yelp. Then another one, a little bit longer. A spotlight shone on us. I froze.

A bullhorn blared out, "DROP WHAT'S IN YOUR HANDS AND STAY WHERE YOU ARE!"

Yelling with all his might, Hernan shouted out, "BEAT IT GUYS!" and we all dropped our cans and started running. We took off, heading back the way we came.

"SPREAD OUT!" Cisco commanded, and we all started zig-zagging through the trash, rocks, and tumbleweeds.

The spotlight was still on us. I didn't have any trouble seeing in front of me. Then I heard a familiar noise behind me. The thundering *chop-chop-chop* sound was unmistakable. I turned to look behind me and I saw a sheriff helicopter flying low just above the bridge. There was a squad car sitting atop the bridge with a couple of cops standing with spotlights, too. I turned my head and just kept running. I jumped over rocks and tumbleweeds like I was jumping hurdles at a track meet. Every now and then I'd come up on one of the guys and then I'd dart away to keep moving in a different direction. I heard one of the guys fall and curse, but I didn't turn around to see who it was. Soon there were no lights anymore and I was running in the dark, but I just kept moving. Out of breath, I saw the gates to the wash just ahead in the distance. Hernan had beaten me back; I saw him climbing up the embankment, with a few steps behind. I heard sounds behind me, too, so I knew I wasn't last.

I ran up the embankment and leaped onto the fence. I climbed and hopped over the top as if hungry wolves were chasing me. When I got down on the other side, Hernan and Ferdinand were already there, hunched over, huffing and puffing. Then I heard Bartolomeu, Nando, and Cisco scurrying up the embankment. In seconds, they were over the fence and with us. You could have heard our hearts pounding from a block away.

Slowly at first, and then picking up momentum, we all began laughing, like that night at the park.

Hernan finally spoke. "All right. We split up and go home."

And that's what we did.

I started out walking casually, but when I got a block or so away from the guys I started running again. A part of me thought the cops might still be after us. I even thought that they might be at my abuela's by the time I got there, telling her everything, as she shook her head and cried. That would be horrible.

When I got back to my block, everything looked the same as when I'd left. There were still a few cars rolling around the neighborhood, and the music and parties were still going on. I had forgotten to put on my watch, so I wondered how long I'd been out.

When I got to my front door, I feared for a second that I might have lost my key in the wash. Luckily I found it in my back pocket. I was surprised to see that the lights were still out inside the house. As I opened the door, I peered inside through the darkness for the figure of my abuela. But no one was waiting for me. I closed the door and tiptoed up the stairs. I looked down the hall and saw the sliver of light under my abuela's door, just like it had been when I had left.

Inside my room, I closed the door and undressed. After climbing into bed, I looked at the clock on my nightstand. It read 3:15. As I pulled the covers up around me, I could feel my heart still pounding away. Whew, I thought. If my abuela had caught me out this late she would have killed me for sure. If the cops had caught us I'd be twice dead. I was lucky this time, real lucky.

Chapter 4

BECAUSE MY ABUELA ALWAYS SEEMED to to know when I did something wrong, I tried to stay away from her all weekend long. I just gamed most of the time and went to the park to play soccer in the afternoons. I kept thinking that maybe she knew I'd snuck out and that she was just letting the guilt eat me up before punishing me. As we rode to church on Sunday morning, I tried to act normal. But when we made the turn to pass the gates of the wash on our way to the freeway, I got nervous. I guess my abuela noticed. "What's the matter with you?" she asked.

"Nothing," I replied, and she left it alone.

Even though Hernan had put the word out that nobody was to talk about what had happened at the wash Friday night, by the time we got to school Monday morning, everybody knew. All the Conquistadors had a kind of gleam in their eyes like they were proud that everybody knew because it made us look cool. I didn't feel the same way.

With so many people knowing that we went down to the wash, I figured it wouldn't be long before the principal found out. During homeroom announcements, the principal mentioned that the sheriff's department had issued a warning to all area schools that the wash was dangerous and that it was illegal to trespass there. I kept my head low and pretended to read, but a few of the kids turned around and started to razz Ferdinand and me. I ignored them and hoped the teacher wouldn't notice, and luckily she didn't.

That's another thing I realized about middle school: You can't keep a secret. Even when everybody agrees something's supposed to be a secret, it's just a matter of time before it gets out. And the more important it is, the quicker it gets out. The best thing to do is to keep it a secret between you and yourself. That way, if it does get out, you know who to blame.

Lucky for me that wasn't the only talk that Monday morning. The big news of the day was that we were having our fall dance Thursday night. By lunchtime nobody was talking about the wash anymore. It was all dance this, dance that, and dance-dance-dance.

I'd never been to a dance before, so I didn't know how to feel about it. We'd had little lunchtime sock hops back in second grade, but that was years ago. Nobody knew how to dance then, so nobody knew how bad you danced. Now everybody would be able to see. And then there was the whole question of who would dance with whom. Back in second grade it didn't matter that all the guys danced with guys and all the girls danced with girls. But now eighth graders would be there and that meant there would be girl and guy dancing. All the girls seemed happy that there was a dance coming up, but most of the guys were nervous like me.

Walking home that afternoon, I quizzed the other guys on what they knew about dancing. They were in the dark like me, except for Hernan. He knew some old-school break dance moves and he showed us a couple. They looked pretty good, but he couldn't go to the dance anyway because he was on behavior probation at school. Same with Bartolomeu, and Cisco was on academic probation for bad grades, so he couldn't go either. That left just Ferdinand, Nando, and me from the Conquistadors.

I went straight to the TV when I got home, and turned on lots of music videos. My abuela wondered what was up because I usually did my homework first, *then* gamed. I told her about the dance on Thursday and how I didn't know how. She got all silly and started laughing. She showed me some dances that she used to do from the sixties and seventies. Then she made me practice the box step with her; she said they might play a slow song, and that's what they danced at the Catholic school she'd gone to when she was my age. I told her that nobody danced like that anymore and that I'd look stupid doing that Thursday night. We practiced the box step anyway, but we sure didn't look like anything I'd ever seen on TV.

As the days headed up to the dance, things got stranger and stranger. The girls at school started acting weird and would look at us guys funny, like they were judging us or something. Then they'd turn back to their little groups and start laughing real loud. Henrietta even started staring at me in class. She was in most of my classes and she kept looking over at me like she was waiting for me to say something. Normally I would just say "Hey" and "What's up," but this felt different. I just turned away from her when I noticed her staring.

All week long I went straight home after school to watch music videos. I had one or two dance steps down pretty good, and I learned how to do the Soulja dance—but everybody knew that one. When Thursday finally came, it was one of the quietest days I could remember at school. Guys would pass girls and turn away quickly. Girls would pass guys and cling closer to their little packs of girls. The only people that were loose and carefree were Hernan, Cisco, and Bartolomeu, probably because they couldn't go to the dance. All day I got sick to my stomach just thinking about the dance. I thought about ditching it altogether, but Ferdinand and Nando were going, and I figured they would need my support as much as I needed theirs.

And even though Hernan, Cisco, and Bartolomeu weren't going to the actual dance, they had plans of their own. Every afternoon that week, while I was practicing dance moves, they were roaming around the neighborhood looking for illegal fireworks.

Illegal fireworks aren't hard to find except when you really need them. That's what the guys were finding out. It seemed like somebody was always going to Mexico to get them; on the Fourth of July you can hear and see them everywhere. But though Hernan and the other Conquistadors followed up on every hint, rumor, and lead they had, they still came up with nothing. Finally Cisco suggested they ask Henrietta's pop and they got lucky. When he popped open the trunk of his old hot rod, there was every kind of illegal firework they could think of inside. They got cherry bombs, M-80s, Roman candles, everything, all for twenty bucks. While they were there, they even got tattoos. The guys had liked my tag of the helmet, so all of them got one tattooed on the soft part of their hands between their thumbs and index fingers.

When they showed me their tattoos on Thursday afternoon, I started to feel miserable because I knew that meant I had to get one, too. I told them, "Cool. Awesome." And, "Mine's next." But inside I was thinking that I wished this whole Conquistador thing had never happened, that I'd never answered, "The

Conquistadors," when that girl had asked us what we called ourselves that one day at lunch. I wished my tag hadn't been their favorite.

When I got home my abuela had dinner waiting for me. Asada tacos. Usually I would've eaten maybe five because they were so delicious, but I tried to eat just two, and I couldn't even taste them. I was too nervous. I didn't want my abuela to think I was nervous, but she knew anyway.

"Don't worry about it, Manny. You're going to have fun. Dances are lots of fun."

I just nodded.

After dinner I went up to my room to change for the dance. Normally I didn't think much about clothes. Back in elementary school, dressing had been easy; we had uniforms. Now I just wore what was clean. For school I had three shirts and three pairs of jeans. And for church I had a white long sleeved shirt and a pair of dark pants. And of course the Conquistadors always wore a white T-shirts and unwashed jeans, so I had those, too. But I had no idea of what to wear for a dance. My church shirt or one of my school shirts? My church pants or my Conquistador jeans? When I got upstairs to my room, I discovered that my abuela had helped me out already.

Laid out on my bed was a silver shirt. It was long sleeved and it shimmered. My abuela had kept all of Vasco's clothes from when he was a baby, all the way up through high school. This was one of his old shirts from when he was a freshman in high school. It was made of silk and looked really expensive.

"You like it?"

I turned around to find my abuela standing in the doorway, smiling.

"Wow. That's cool."

"Vasco wore it to some of his dances."

"It's nice. You think he'd get mad?"

My abuela giggled softly for a moment. "No. That shirt is the last thing on his mind right now," my abuela said, making the sign of the cross. "He'd want you to wear it."

"Okay. Thanks."

Now that I had Vasco's shirt to borrow, it was easier to get dressed. But first, before I put on my clothes, I washed up real good. I used the coconut soap my abuela left out for company and washed my face and hands real clean. I even scrubbed under my fingernails so they looked neat. And even though I wasn't old enough to shave, I put on a splash of Vasco's blue velvet aftershave so I would smell nice. Then I put on my clothes. I started out with my regular school blue jeans, but the silk shirt looked too nice for them, so I put on my Conquistador unwashed blue jeans. The shirt still looked too nice, so I put on my dark church pants instead. As for shoes, I went ahead and put my church shoes on, too, so I would look cool from head to toe. After I finished, I took a look at myself in the long bathroom mirror.

Wow, I thought. Something about the clothes makes me look older. I wondered if anybody else would notice.

The dance started at six-thirty and it was already five forty-five. Ready or not, it was time to go. All dressed up, I hopped down the stairs. My abuela was waiting for me at the door with one of those old instant cameras that the picture pops out of.

"Ah. Look at the Chico-Suave!" she teased.

"Come on. I got to go. I got to meet the guys on the corner at six."

"Wait—wait—wait. I have to take your picture."

My abuela made me pose on the stairs. She wouldn't let me leave until the picture came out. Then she wanted to take another one. I stopped rushing her. She was having so much fun. I didn't want to take that away from her.

"Ah. Your mama and papa are going to cry when they see you all dressed up like that."

I kissed her on the cheek, then took off down the street. Starting to get nervous again, I thought I might still ditch the dance and go find Hernan and the other guys. They were going to pull something with those fireworks they'd bought—that might be more fun than the dance. Then I saw Nando and Ferdinand standing on the corner waiting for me. I knew I couldn't turn back.

Nando and Ferdinand were all dressed up, too. They had on black long sleeved shirts and church shoes. We started to goof and clown each other right away, which made us feel less anxious. By the time we got to the school we were all feeling psyched.

Things were pretty busy in front of the school. You could hear the music from the parking lot, and there were some parents and teachers standing around as chaperones. The principal was at the front door greeting the kids as they came in. As we passed him he nodded and said hi to Ferdinand and Nando, but stumbled over my name. I was actually relieved. It was never a good thing to have a principal know you by name.

Inside the auditorium it looked like a big party was going on. The teachers had decorated everything with streamers and balloons. One of the music teachers was the DJ, and there was even a disco ball hanging from the ceiling. There were long tables covered with trays of small sandwiches, cookies, chips, and punch. All the guys had on nice pants and dress shirts, and all the girls were wearing dresses and skirts. I was surprised, because some of the girls I'd never seen in anything but jeans and T-shirts. Some of them looked pretty cool.

Nando and Ferdinand went straight to the food tables, and I followed them. They hadn't eaten dinner yet, so they filled their plates up with sandwiches and ate them two at a time. I grabbed a cup of punch. It tasted pretty good. For some reason, party punch always tastes better than the punch you get at home. I looked around the auditorium. Some kids were already dancing, mostly eighth graders. My class, the seventh graders, pretty much just stood around and watched the eighth graders dance. A few of them could dance pretty well. I wondered how bad I'd look if I went out there. Everybody would probably laugh. I drank some more punch and looked around for a place to sit. There were a few tables with chairs by the dance floor. I spotted an empty table and waved over the guys.

The first twenty minutes or so of the dance were pretty uneventful. Some kids danced. Some just ate. The guys and I just watched and made fun of any guy we knew who got out on the floor and danced. When my geeky friend Nicky got out on the dance floor with some blonde eighth-grade girl, we almost fell out of our chairs laughing. He didn't care. He looked over at us and tried to act all gangster-style, which made us laugh even harder. But he danced pretty good.

I started to think that that's all that dances were, getting up from the table to get punch, saying hi to people, and joking around with your friends. I was on about my fourth cup of punch when I noticed a table of girls sitting near us. They were pretty much doing what me and the guys were doing, watching the eighth graders dance and making fun of any classmates who had enough nerve to get out on the dance floor. One of the girls was Henrietta. And every time I looked in that direction, she was staring at me, like she'd been doing in class all week. I wondered what it meant. Then out of nowhere, she got up and walked over to our table. Everything seemed to move in slow motion.

"So are you going to dance with me, Manny?"

"Huh?" I heard what she said the first time, but "huh" came out of my mouth. I didn't know what to do. I was scared, but I couldn't let the guys think so. As she said the words again, it felt like my throat dropped into my stomach. My heart started beating like it was trying to find a way out of my chest. I could feel my pulse on my eardrums and then I couldn't hear anything. I didn't even hear myself saying, "All right, girl."

I tried to act cool, but it was like I was in a dream. I could see myself getting up from the table and walking out onto the dance floor with Henrietta, but I didn't feel like I was inside my body. I don't know when it happened, but somewhere between the dance floor and the table Henrietta and I started holding hands. By the time we got out on the dance floor my hand was wet with sweat. Hers was too, so I thought it must be normal. Then Henrietta let go of my hand and started to dance. I didn't dare look back at the table. I knew the guys were watching and laughing. I knew I looked stupid just standing there, so I figured I'd better dance. For the life of me I couldn't remember any of the steps that I'd practiced all week. I just started to move. I knew I looked stupid but I just kept going. Then little by little I started to remember the dance moves I'd learned from the music videos. After a minute or so, I was doing the dances I had learned and they felt pretty good. I looked up at Henrietta and she was smiling. It wasn't like she was smiling because I looked stupid. It looked like she was smiling because she liked dancing with me. So I smiled too.

My abuela was right, I thought. Dances were fun. Henrietta and I danced for a long time, maybe five songs. Then they played a slow song and I didn't know what to do. I looked around and saw the eighth graders starting to dance real close. I was too scared to dance that close to Henrietta. Then I remembered the old box step my grandma had taught me. I showed it to Henrietta and she started laughing, so we tried that dance for a while. Then we just held hands and moved side to side. The chaperones were checking the dance floor to see if any kids were dancing too close, and they were busting and benching the kids they caught. But the slow song soon ended, and the Soulja Boy song came on. That's when the dance really took off.

You could tell that everybody loved the Soulja dance. Everybody cheered and started doing the steps. I looked over at the table for Nando and Ferdinand, but they had found partners and were doing the dance, too. It seemed like the whole room was dancing. Then it happened. From out of nowhere, two ear-blasting *kabooms* seemed to shake the auditorium. After a split second of shock, I realized what it was. Another loud *kaboom* sounded outside. The lights went out in the auditorium and the safety lights came on. Then the fire bells started ringing. The Principal rushed onto the dance floor with a bullhorn.

"Listen up. Everybody out on the football field. Line up like ladies and gentlemen and go out the double doors in back," the principal instructed.

Nando and Ferdinand looked over at me with big grins. I

grinned and nodded back. We knew what the explosions were and who had caused them. Just then another *kaboom* sounded out.

It was dark outside on the football field. Just like during a regular school-day fire drill, kids were standing around laughing and joking. Henrietta went back to her little girl-pack of friends. I looked around for signs of Hernan, Cisco, and Bartolomeu. Suddenly a loud whistle rang out. I looked up, and a Roman candle exploded in the sky. Then another whistled and exploded, and then another. *Kaboom!* They were coming from all directions. The guys must have been at different positions—one on the street that ran on the right of the school, another on the street to the left of the school, and another down the embankment of the wash. The fireworks kept going. It was too dark to see anybody lighting them. *Kaboom! Wheee! Boom!*

It was a nice show for a couple of minutes. Then I heard whistles of another kind. They were the sounds of sirens in the distance. After one last *kaboom* the fireworks stopped. The sirens were the only sounds in the night. Soon we could see flashing red and blue lights near the school parking lot. Nando, Ferdinand, and I tried not to look at each other. I don't think any of us wanted to get into trouble. After a few minutes the principal came out onto the football field and told everyone to go home. The dance was over.

Since Henrietta lived near us, she decided to walk home with Nando, Ferdinand, and me. We counted three fire trucks and five police cars in the parking lot. The Conquistadors had really made a scene tonight, I thought.

The guys didn't mention the fireworks the whole walk home with Henrietta. When we got to her block, she gave me a kiss on the cheek goodnight and then went home.

"Bye. I'll see you in school tomorrow."

"All right, girl," I said real coolly, 'cause the guys were watching.

The guys teased me some on the way to my block about how I had a girlfriend, but I didn't care. Henrietta and I had had fun. The guys were worried some about the trouble we might get into because of the fireworks, so we all agreed not to say anything.

Chapter 5

THE FIREWORKS HAD A BIGGER impact than the Conquistadors could have ever imagined. Hernan, Cisco, and Bartolomeu didn't get caught, and nobody ratted them out, but now there were always cop cars outside school when school got out, going up and down the street to keep an eye on the kids. A couple of times they even drove slowly behind the guys and me as we walked home. Hernan would taunt them to make us laugh as they drove behind us. He'd curse at them in Spanish and pretend like he had an emergency and needed help. I just laughed when the other guys laughed and played along so I didn't look weak.

Over Thanksgiving break I tried to avoid the guys as much as I could. After soccer in the afternoons, I would tell them I had to go straight home because I was on restriction. I really wasn't on restriction but they didn't know that, and I doubted they would ask my abuela. At home I mostly just gamed up in my room or I'd watch TV with my abuela. Every now and then she'd ask me what was up, and how come I wasn't playing with my friends. I would tell her they all had to do homework or that I was waiting for a call from Henrietta. When I'd say that, she'd get all giggly but I didn't care. I just wanted to stay out of trouble.

The week before Christmas break, the gang almost got busted again. It started when Howard, a kid in our class, got his brother's old mp3 player. We're not supposed to bring those things to school, but some kids do anyway. He showed it around and people thought it was pretty cool. When he showed it to me, I told him it was cool, too, but I was really thinking that I never liked those things anyway. With the earplugs in your ears you can't hear anything. But Cisco liked it so much he asked Howard if he could borrow it. Then, when Howard wanted it back, Cisco acted like he didn't know what he was talking about. Howard got so mad he went to the principal's office and made a complaint. When the principal asked him who had it, he didn't just say Cisco. He said the Conquistadors. Then he named us all to the principal, and that's when things got bad. For the first time, we were on record for being a gang.

Almost every day that week I was called into the principal's office for questioning. Was I member of a gang? Was I a member of the Conquistadors? Who's in the Conquistadors? Had I seen the mp3 player? Had I played with the mp3 player? Had I taken the mp3 player? Did I know who had the mp3 player? Did I know what was going to happen to me if I took it and didn't give it back? All that just for a mp3 player.

By Wednesday, I knew none of the Conquistadors was saying anything about the mp3 player. Why else would the office keep calling me in for questioning? And I kept seeing Cisco going to his classes, which meant he wasn't suspended yet. Of course I couldn't say anything, because I didn't really know much about it. I never saw Cisco actually borrow the mp3 player from Howard. I had just heard about it so I didn't really know if that was the real story or not. I couldn't find out what really happened because the guys and I weren't walking home together. Most of the Conquistadors had detention that week, and those that didn't, had tutoring. So every afternoon, the week before Christmas break, I walked home with Henrietta.

Henrietta was a pretty cool girl. She had long black hair and big brown eyes. I got the sense that she was shy with most people until she got to know them. After that she could talk your ear off. Sometimes she'd tell me about what classes she liked and didn't like. She thought my friends were obnoxious, but I felt that way sometimes, too, so that didn't bother me. Occasionally she'd talk about her mom and pop. I got the feeling that she really loved her mom, but thought her pop was crazy. Most people thought that about him, too. I didn't know if it was cool to agree or disagree, so I just kept quiet. Every day that we walked home, right before we got to her block, she would put lip gloss on and then kiss me good-bye on the cheek. I knew if the Conquistadors had seen it they'd laugh their heads off. But it didn't bother me.

The week went smoothly until Friday afternoon. It was the last day before Christmas break. Everybody was excited. No school for two and a half weeks. Some classes that day had problems. There were a few subs working, and for some reason, when a sub is in the class, everybody thinks they have a free pass to goof off. Kids who would never get into trouble with a regular teacher all of a sudden do stupid things. Nicky, who's a straight-up geek, decided to get mouthy with a sub in first period. By second period he was in the principal's office. A couple of girls wouldn't shut up in second period and they got sent out, too. By fourth period PE, there were ten kids missing that I had seen in first period.

With all that had happened that week—from Howard's mp3 player turning up missing to me getting sent to the principal's office for questioning—I just wanted the day to end. When the sub for my last period science class put in a movie, I thought I'd relax, watch the video, and wait out the clock. But some kids started throwing stuff and cutting up, even with the movie on. The sub called security and sent out five kids. I thought it was plain *stupid* to get in trouble an hour before Christmas break. I guess all the Conquistadors were thinking like me because none of them got into trouble that Friday. Even Hernan was cool. He knew a good thing when he saw it. And having detention the day before Christmas break was not a good thing.

Hernan had something on his mind. I didn't know it, but he and Cisco were planning something for Howard. Hernan had been holding a grudge all week. In his eyes being a rat was the worst thing a guy could do. "You don't rat. And you especially don't rat on Conquistadors," he would say. And even though the principal couldn't figure out exactly what happened to Howard's mp3 player, he was looking in our direction, and Hernan didn't like that.

Like I had for most of the week, I walked home with Henrietta that Friday. The guys were walking about half a block ahead. Every now and then one of them would turn around and yell back to us, "Hey! You and your *wife* are walking too slow!" Then they'd turn around and laugh their heads off. Henrietta and I couldn't help but laugh, too. It *was* kind of funny. But it didn't bother us. Henrietta was all happy about Christmas coming up. Her grandmas and grandpas and cousins and aunts and uncles were all coming over to her house for a big party. She said she always got tons of presents, and there would be lots of food and games. It sounded nice. She even invited me to come over, and

I told her maybe. I wasn't sure what I wanted to do for Christmas. Maybe my abuela might be sad that Vasco was in jail, and I wouldn't want to leave her alone like that.

I hadn't noticed that the guys were trailing Howard by half a block or so. Howard was walking with Nicky, and they didn't seem to notice anything odd. Then I heard the call.

"*Get him, guys!*" Hernan shouted out.

Howard heard the call and turned around. The Conquistadors ran full speed down the street after him. I could see Howard looked scared from where I was standing, half a block away. He fumbled with his backpack and just froze up. Quickly the guys surrounded him. I could hear Hernan and Cisco yelling something at him. Then they were pushing and shoving him around. It wouldn't be much of fight, I thought. Howard had probably never thrown a hand at anybody in his life. I felt sorry for him. I wanted to run up there and help him, but I just walked along with Henrietta. The guys all knew that Howard was a geek and probably couldn't fight, I decided. So maybe they were just going to scare him a little a bit. Then I saw it with my own eyes. Hernan hauled off and socked Howard in the mouth. Cisco was standing just behind Howard and nailed him on the cheek. Bartolomeu took his turn and started punching Howard in the stomach. Howard would've fallen to the ground, but there were too many Conquistadors keeping him up.

I almost jumped in my shoes when I heard the loud yelp of a siren. I turned to look, and a cop car whizzed right in front of me. It raced by Henrietta and me and went directly to the curb where the guys were. The guys took off in all directions. Even Howard took off this time. The only person who didn't run was Nicky, who had somehow fallen into some bushes during the melee.

By the time Henrietta and I walked past the scene, the cop was out of his car and questioning Nicky. I could hear Nicky say, "I didn't see anything. I don't know who they are. Maybe they're high schoolers or something." Nicky knew the rules, I thought. You don't rat, no matter what. He didn't even say anything to me as Henrietta and I walked by. He glanced quickly at us, then turned the other way.

The cop turned away from Nicky to ask Henrietta and me, "Did you see what happened?"

Coolly I replied, "*¡No, no hablamos inglés!*"

The cop was white, so I knew we had a chance that he didn't speak Spanish and wouldn't want to bother with us. The cop quickly turned back to Nicky. Henrietta and I walked on down the street.

We were a block away before Henrietta said, "Your friends are crazy."

"I know. They're out of control."

"You should get some new friends."

"We've been friends since kindergarten. They're the only friends I've ever had."

"They're going to get you in trouble."

"They're already getting me in trouble," I told her. "I spent all week going in and out of the principal's office. He used to not know my name. Now he thinks I'm in a gang."

"You *are* in a gang," Henrietta said.

"Not really. It's not a real gang."

"What is it then? You do crazy stuff. You take things that aren't yours. You beat people up."

"*I* don't," I defended myself.

"Your friends do. You are who your friends are, Manny."

Henrietta was right, I thought, but I didn't want to say it to her face. I knew what she meant, how I'm a part of it even if I'm not. And maybe she was a little shook up over seeing Howard getting beat up. Whatever it was, she didn't kiss me on the cheek when we stopped at her block, like she'd done all week long. But she did invite me again to her house for Christmas. I told her maybe, and left it open.

Chapter 6

THE THINGS I LIKED BEST about Christmas were the tamales. My abuela makes the best ones. Ever since I can remember, we had them for the holidays. They weren't like the ones you get all year long. They were special. Throughout the year when my abuela made them, she would use pork and rice, but for Christmas she would make them with chicken, green chilies, and black beans. They were so delicious I could eat them for breakfast, lunch, and dinner, two or three at a time. My abuela sold them all through the holidays. For two weeks people would be knocking on the door to get her Christmas tamales. It made me proud that so many people thought my abuela's tamales were the best.

During the holidays, my abuela would start her day at five in the morning. She'd begin by making a pot of homemade chocolate and pan dulce fresh every day that was just for us. When I woke up that's what we'd have to eat. Abuela would say that when she smelled chocolate and pan dulce in the kitchen, that's what made her feel like cooking. Then she would plug in four electric crockpots that she had just for the chicken. She would season the chicken and cook it for six hours until the meat fell off the bone. While the chicken cooked, she'd take the soaking cornhusks and lay them out in large pans. She'd mix the masa in huge mixing bowls. My abuela's masa was always smooth, never lumpy. Then she'd open the big cans of black beans, and say with a smile, "Don't tell anyone I use beans from a can. It doesn't taste any different." I would nod and say "okay," but nobody ever asked anyway.

After that my abuela grated the Jack cheese and got the green chilies from the refrigerator. Finally, after stripping all the bones from the chicken, she was ready to roll the tamales. She used a large spoon to scoop up the masa and smear it onto the cornhusks. She would then scoop on the chicken, beans, and grated cheese, and place a long green chili on top. She then rolled each husk tightly and steamed the tamales in two big army pots. You could smell them steaming all over the neighborhood.

I didn't see much of the guys over the holidays. Although Cisco and Bartolomeu came over a couple of times to game, that's all we did—game. We didn't talk about the Conquistadors. We just gamed. It was kind of nice. It reminded me of what it was like before we became the Conquistadors. One thing stuck out the whole time: Hernan wasn't there. If he had been, I'm sure he would've figured out some way for us all to get into trouble. Luckily he was working with his uncle.

Hernan's uncle was a plumber. He did really well. He had a new truck and a house and family. When Hernan wasn't in school, or when he was on vacation, he was his uncle's helper for twenty dollars a day. Hernan's dad was in prison so Hernan gave the money he made to his mom to help out. I thought that was pretty cool of him. It made him seem so much older than we were. That was the good side of Hernan.

The bad side of Hernan was something I really couldn't understand. He could be bossy. He had these rules that he thought we should go by, but he didn't like to be told what to do. It always amazed me how much energy Hernan could spend on not doing his classwork or homework when he was the type of guy who could finish it all in about ten minutes. When most kids could only do math one way, Hernan could solve problems four or five different ways. But to Hernan, school was for wimps. It just wasn't macho. I think he mostly got those ideas from his brothers. I thought it was kind of stupid to get ideas from people who were in prison, but to Hernan, those ideas were the only real ideas. The rest of life was stupid.

And then there was the crazy side of Hernan. I'd seen it every now and then since I'd known him, but once the Conquistadors got started, it became a regular thing. He'd get angry and have to hit something or somebody. He would start a fight with anybody just to start a fight. This careless anger made him cool to the other guys.

I didn't talk about this to the guys. I didn't want them to think that I was betraying Hernan. Hernan was still my friend, but he was becoming a hard friend to have. When we were all together as the Conquistadors, they were all becoming hard friends to have. If Hernan was angry, pretty soon everyone wanted to fight and do stupid things. I didn't want to be known as a gangster. But they did.

Henrietta called me every day over the holidays. My abuela would get all giggly and smile whenever she would brought the phone to me.

"Maannnny, it's your girrrrllfriend!" she'd sing.

I never knew what it meant to have a girlfriend, so I didn't know what to say on the phone with her. We mostly asked each other what we were doing. What we were eating. Did one or the other like this or that. It was kind of cool to find out so much about another person, especially a girl. I'd always wondered what they were thinking and if they thought the same things that guys thought. I learned that they didn't game as much as we did. That they read books more than we did. That they liked to listen to music. That they liked to be just on the phone just to be on the phone. With guys, if they called, it was to the point—get the information, and then see you there and bye. With Henrietta, it was like, now that we're on the phone, let's just stay on the phone until something interesting comes up for us to say. Sometimes there were these long breaks during our talks that made me wonder if I was supposed to say bye and hang up, or if I was supposed to stay on the phone. I always had to make sure I used the bathroom and had a good drink of water before she called because she could stay on the phone for a half hour or more.

I also learned from Henrietta that once a girl wants you to do something, they don't stop asking until you do it. For a week and a half, since before Christmas break started, she'd been asking me to come to her family's Christmas party. I wasn't sure that I wanted to go so I kept telling her maybe. But every day that she called, she'd bring it up again. On the day before Christmas Eve I finally gave in and told her, yeah, I'd go—just so she wouldn't bring it up again. Right after I regretted it. I wasn't even at the party yet, and I already had that uncomfortable feeling of being in a room full of strange grown-ups and having to be polite and worrying about doing the wrong thing. It wasn't like the dance. This time I'd be there all by myself; Henrietta and her drunk pop were the only two people that I'd know. The only thing I could think of was to make my abuela go to the party with me.

She'd known Henrietta's family for years, and there'd be other abuelas there. She'd fit in better than me.

Christmas Eve turned out really nice. My abuela cooked tamales all day as usual but she baked special sweets too. After dinner we had apple pie with eggnog. The whole house smelled like cinnamon and spice. The tree was all lit up. There was music playing throughout the house. And even though I was too old for the Santa Claus story my abuela still tried to con me.

"Santa said he's going to be really busy this year, Manny, so he's not sure that he can make it to our house. He said he knows you're a good person and will understand if he misses our house and visits a kid who really needs a gift," she said.

My abuela said this every year to make me realize that some kids didn't have as much as I did. It always made me feel guilty. I hated to think of kids out there who didn't have food or a blanket or something to play with. But I knew they were out there. Some of the kids at school didn't have game boxes or enough clothes or anything. So I said the same thing to my abuela every year, even though I knew there'd be presents under the tree in the morning.

"It's okay, Nana. I know."

My mom and pop called me on Christmas Eve. We hadn't talked for a long time, so it felt good to hear from them. We talked about how school was going and if I had everything I needed. I told them I loved them and that everything was good. If my pop had been with me in person, I might have asked him what I should do about the Conquistadors. But since I was on the phone and my abuela was standing nearby, I didn't say anything.

After the call, I pretty much stayed up in my room gaming for the rest of the night. I tried not to think about going over to Henrietta's for the party. I was starting to learn that the more you thought about something, the more nervous it could make you. My abuela had agreed to come with me, so I wasn't going to be alone. She told me if it wasn't fun we could tell them we had somewhere else to go and that we could leave early.

Christmas morning was a blast. My abuela had menudo ready for breakfast when I woke up. We ate and then we opened up presents. I got my abuela this yellow bath salt that smelled like perfume from the drugstore, and when she opened it she was so happy she started to cry. If I had known what she was going to get me I would have got her two or three more gifts, because she really came through. I guess she didn't know that some games were strictly for grown-ups, because she got me the first three versions of Carjack. I couldn't it believe when I opened up the box. I was almost too embarrassed to take the games out.

"Nana! Are you sure?" I asked her.

"The man at the store said that's the game all the kids want to play."

I was learning fast when to use a little white lie. When my abuela asked me what the game was about, I told her I play a cop and I'm trying to catch some car thieves. The truth was, *I* was the car thief. I couldn't tell if she believed me or not. But she seemed happy that I was happy. And I was happy that she was so happy. And it was Christmas, so the truth didn't seem to matter.

One last package was still lying under the tree. It was long and wide and wrapped strangely because of its awkward shape.

"Wait-wait! There's one more left," my abuela excitedly said.

"That one's for me?" I asked, feeling that I'd gotten enough already.

"It says Manny on the card," answered my abuela.

I picked up the odd present. It was kind of heavy and yet kind of light at the same time. I hadn't asked for anything that looked like something of this shape, I thought. I tore into the wrapping paper. I was shocked. It was a skateboard. I knew my abuela was watching, so I smiled and thanked her. I lied and told her it was cool, but I wondered what had made her buy me a skateboard.

To be honest, skaters weren't liked at my school. They had their own clique, the skater clique. They wore black all the time, kept their hair long, and listened to alternative rock. They rode their boards to school and carried them around all day long. Then they rode home on them and did tricks on the sidewalks. And there I was on Christmas morning, sitting on the floor with a new skateboard. Funny, I thought, because I could imagine myself as anything, even the geekiest geek, but never, ever, as a skater dude.

I helped my abuela clean up the mess on the floor, grabbed up my new games, and went up to my room. As I was walking up the stairs, my abuela called out, "Manny. Don't forget your skateboard."

I walked back downstairs and got the board.

All Christmas morning I played Carjack. I turned the volume down to low so my abuela wouldn't hear the game. Even the sounds and language were bad. But it was a fun game. At one o'clock I remembered that I had to get dressed for Henrietta's party. My abuela and I were supposed to be there by two. So I stopped playing and got my clothes out. Once again, I didn't know what to wear. Vasco's shirt, that I'd worn for the fall dance, seemed too flashy for a neighborhood party. I chose my church clothes without the tie. I took a bath, threw on my clothes, and met my abuela downstairs.

My abuela was all dressed up. It was a surprise to see her like that. Except for church, all she wore were housedresses, and they all looked alike. She seemed really happy to be going out. Usually the only places she went to were the grocery store, the drug store, and church meetings. If he wasn't in solitary, she went to see Vasco once a month. But lately he'd been getting into trouble in prison and couldn't have visitors.

We walked over to the party and got there right on time. It looked like the party had been going on for a while. There were cars parked all up and down the street. The garage door was open and the men were outside in the garage drinking beer and listening to music. Little kids, all dressed up, were running all over the place. Everybody had plates of food. Henrietta's pop and the other men greeted us as we walked through the garage to enter the house. They looked like they had been drinking for a long time. They were sweaty and red-faced, and their eyes looked glossed over. Some of them knew my abuela and hugged and kissed her. They even offered her a beer. I was surprised when my abuela took it and thanked them—but she's such a lady that she wrapped a paper towel around the can before drinking from it. A lady should never be seen drinking in public, she liked to say. She's old-fashioned like that.

Inside the house there were tons of people chatting and laughing. Babies were crying. There were so many sounds I didn't know what to listen to. Henrietta's mom was wearing a traditional poblano skirt and blouse, as were some of the other women. Even Henrietta's baby sister had a folk dress on. There was food everywhere. Tamales. Carne asada. Enchiladas. Chips. Salsa. And a great big bowl of punch with sliced fruit in it. The women greeted my abuela with hugs and kisses. They complimented each other and then pinched my cheeks and said, "Ahhh. Look at the little man of the house!" I felt so embarrassed. They made me feel like I was five years old again.

The biggest surprise of the party for me was how Henrietta

looked. She wore a matching skirt like her mom's and her hair was pulled back real tight into a bun. She even had makeup on. I'd never seen her look prettier. She was on the patio in the backyard with a group of her cousins, singing with a karaoke machine. They were laughing like crazy and having great time. When she saw me in the house she ran inside and pulled me outside with her. I didn't know what to do or how to act. She introduced me to her girl cousins, who were all about her age. And then she said it.

"This is my boyfriend, Manuel."

She said it about five times, as she had to repeat herself to each of her cousins.

Even though my skin was brown and couldn't blush much, my face felt like it was the color of a fire engine.

When Henrietta and her cousins started to sing a new song, I found a place to sit at a table on the patio. I decided to stay there for the party. Every fifteen minutes or so Henrietta's mom or Henrietta herself would bring me something from the kitchen. I must've drunk twenty cups of punch and eaten a dozen or so different kinds of pastries. I had a plate of enchiladas plus five or six flautas. I had bowls of chips with salsa and more candy than I'd eaten all year long. By the time the sun went down I was so full my belt buckle was jabbing into my stomach.

Then one of the husbands got angry at his wife, and the party came to a halt. The music stopped. People got quiet and serious.

The argument had started inside the garage. The husband was drunk and his wife was mad and crying. They were yelling at each other, while everyone else was trying to calm them down.

Suddenly my abuela was standing next to me. She grabbed my hand firmly in a way that showed me how serious the situation was. She had hardly held my hand since about second grade. And the way she was holding it now was the same way she had grabbed it when I was a baby and was about to do something stupid like walk out into the street.

"Come on, Manny. It's time to go home," she said seriously.

I waved and nodded bye to Henrietta, who waved back to me from inside the house.

I let my abuela guide me onto the front sidewalk, holding my hand the whole time. The man who was fighting with his wife looked wasted. He could hardly stand up. I wondered if that was what being a grown-up was like, getting drunk at parties and having fights with your wife. I could never imagine myself being like that as a grown-up, but maybe he couldn't either, at my age.

"Don't stare, Manny," my abuela said, and she clutched my hand tighter.

She held it the whole way home. When we got inside the house, she sighed, "Whew! That was a good party, huh? The food—oh my goodness!"

A little while later I heard a lot of sirens. I traced the sound to Henrietta's house. It must've been that guy, I thought. Still later that night I heard gunshots from the same direction. They didn't sound like trouble gunshots. They sounded like celebration gunshots so I didn't worry too much about them. Somebody was always shooting off guns on holidays, just for the sound of it. If it hadn't been Christmas, it might have meant trouble. But since it was the holiday, I figured somebody was just trying to say, in their own way, Merry Christmas.

Chapter 7

"MY UNCLE WENT TO JAIL!" Henrietta excitedly said over the phone.

She filled me in on what had happened at the party after my abuela and I had left.

"The cops came and everything. He was so drunk he thought they were priests taking him to church!"

I was playing Carjack now, with the phone up to my ear. Henrietta kept talking. She told me about all the presents she got for Christmas: clothes and games and dolls and books. With my mind on the game, I wasn't paying much attention to what she was saying. Then she said something that made me stop cold. The words took a couple of seconds to sink in. I asked Henrietta to repeat what she had just said. She repeated it verbatim.

"And I can't believe that Ophelia and Victor are dating. Victor got jumped into the Playaz, you know?"

A sense of dread sank into me. Victor was the kid Hernan had socked behind the portables at school. The Playaz was a real gang in the city; not some made-up-wannabe-gang like the Conquistadors.

I started to feel nauseous. I told Henrietta I had something to do and hung up. I crawled onto my bed and closed my eyes. I didn't want to think about Hernan and Cisco and how they would take the news. I'd known them since kindergarten. I knew how they reacted to things. Hernan would hear the news and want to check Victor just for being in a gang that was tougher than the Conquistadors.

I stayed in bed all afternoon. My abuela checked on me a couple of times to see if I was all right. I told her that I had been up all night gaming and that now I was tired. It was New Year's Eve and all I wanted to do was hide in my room, pull down the shades, and hope that my life in the Conquistadors was all a bad dream.

At nine o'clock I went downstairs to watch the ball drop in Times Square for New Year's. As I watched the ball falling, it seemed like my life was crashing down, too. In four days I'd be back in school, a Conquistador again, and enemy of the Playaz. I felt doomed.

"Manny. What's wrong with you?" my abuela asked as I sat on the couch watching the TV. She could tell something wasn't right.

"Nothing, Nana."

"Is it the girl?"

"No."

My abuela smiled, giggled, and then said, "Manny, sometimes people don't act the way you want them to, especially girls. That's just life."

My abuela didn't know how right she was. Except it wasn't Henrietta that wasn't acting the way I wanted. It was me. I wanted to run away. I wanted to go over to Hernan's and Cisco's houses and tell them that I'm out, that I didn't want to be a Conquistador anymore, that I wanted to be Manny again. Manny, the borderline geek who liked doing his homework and getting good grades and staying out of trouble. But I didn't.

Through the whole Conquistadors mess I was discovering something important about time. Like when you knew you had to do something horrible, and really didn't want to do it, time would jump right in your face. And soon you were right in the middle of that something horrible, wondering where did all that time go? That's the way it was with the last four days of Christmas break. They seemed to vanish into thin air and there I was again with my backpack on, walking to school. I didn't want to walk with the guys so I had left real early that morning. I decided I'd hide out in the school library until about ten minutes before class. That way, if there was a fight or something, I wouldn't be there.

I loved libraries. They were quiet. They had thousands of stories in them, all kinds of stories. There were stories of good guys and bad guys, winners and losers, rich people and poor people, foreigners and natives. As I looked around, a cover caught my eye. A man was standing by a pickup truck with his pet dog beside him. The title read *Travels with Charley* by John Steinbeck. I liked Steinbeck, I remembered. I grabbed the book and sat down at a table.

I started reading and got into the book real fast. I kept checking the clock on the wall so I wouldn't get to class late. I started to hear more and more voices and activity outside. I knew school was starting soon. I wondered if I could ditch and just stay in the library all day reading. That's a bad idea, I thought. I'd never ditched before. Ten minutes before class, I dog-eared the page I was on and closed the book. I checked it out at the counter and stuffed it in my backpack. Taking a deep breath, I opened the door and hoped for the best.

The sun was shining. The quad was crowded. Some kids were shooting hoops. The girls were in their little groups, talking. The security guards were walking around and watching the kids. It looked like a regular old school day. I spotted the guys in their usual place, sitting on top of some lunch tables, and I made my way over to them. I decided not to mention anything about Victor to the guys. If they knew already, then I didn't need to say anything. If they didn't know already, then I wasn't going to tell them. I didn't want to start any trouble by setting off the whole thing.

"Yo! Manny! *¿Cómo estás?*" they greeted me when I reached the tables.

"Hey, Manny. What did you do on your break?" one of them asked me.

Hernan shot back with a joke. "He did some home repairs with his wife!"

The guys all laughed.

The guys were laughing and clowning. For a few seconds I thought everything was going to be all right. Maybe they all already knew that Victor was in the Playaz and it was no big deal. But then I heard the words.

"NO WAY!" Cisco shouted out.

The other guys hadn't noticed yet what Cisco had seen. I didn't need to look.

"What?" the guys asked, looking all around.

"Check out that fool."

Cisco pointed across the quad to the other side of the basketball courts. Standing with a group of his friends was Victor. There was nothing unusual about that, except that on top of his head was an orange baseball cap.

"No way!" Hernan said.

"I don't believe it," Ferdinand added.

All of the Conquistadors were awestruck by what Victor had on his head. They all knew what it meant. Because some caps are affiliated with gangs, baseball caps weren't allowed at school, so it was just a matter of time before he'd get caught and have to take it off.

"That fool's gonna get whupped by one of the Playaz for wearing that," Hernan said. "They don't play games."

"He knows that," said Bartolomeu.

"Then he must be in," Ferdindand said.

"They wouldn't let that fool in," Cisco argued.

Ferdinand replied, "Maybe he is. I thought his brother José was one of the Playaz."

"Was he?" Hernan asked. The surprised look of just remembering something shot across his face. "Oh, yeah. Maybe he was. Well, he's still a rat."

I felt a little calmer as Hernan wound down a little. I wondered what he was thinking. But he didn't do anything. He just played it cool. So I did, too.

For the rest of the day Hernan and the Conquistadors played it cool. No matter where we were or what we were doing they would all look around to see if Victor was around. They would watch to see what he was doing and who he was talking to. By second period, he wasn't wearing the orange cap anymore. One of the teachers must have figured out something was up and made him take it off.

Victor had a lot of friends, but his main buddy was Carl. Victor and Carl were friends like Cisco, Hernan, and I were friends. They had gone to elementary school together and had known each other since kindergarten, too. I was friends with them both before the Conquistadors started and Hernan punched Victor. Carl was a good guy. We played Little League together a couple years back. We would trade games with each other and not worry about getting them back because we knew that neither of us would steal from the other. But ever since Hernan and Victor got into it, I hadn't talked to either Victor or Carl.

Carl had a weight problem. He was a lot more than just chubby. We were in seventh grade, and I guessed he must have been at 250 pounds already. He was five or six inches taller than the rest of us, too, which made people think he was a lot older, like a high schooler already. But I think he was a few months younger than me. He really liked to eat. He could eat three lunches in the cafeteria and still be hungry thirty minutes later. He always had candy and snacks hidden in his backpack. Some kids wondered how Carl could afford all that candy. His parents weren't rich. Some others of us knew what he did, but we'd never talk about it because just talking about it could get us into big trouble.

After school Carl walked past the high school on his way home. He knew some of the older kids there, and those older kids always wanted to party. Carl was their connection for herb. He'd carry the little plastic bags of herb in his socks. We'd all heard about drugs from when the cops came and did presentations on just saying no and stuff. We saw drugs on TV all the time, too. And somebody was always getting arrested in town for selling stuff that they shouldn't be selling. My abuela's son Vasco had gotten mixed up with drugs. But Carl never got busted or even suspected of dealing drugs. It was almost like he was too cool about it to get caught. He was just Carl. Big, goofy, always-snacking Carl.

Because Carl was so big and tall, a lot of kids were scared of him. Kids wouldn't even think of trying to fight him because he looked like he could brush off anything. The coach was always trying to get Carl to play football for the school team, but he wouldn't do it. He once told me that afternoon practice would mess up his business. He had to be around the high school after school. And now Carl was essentially Victor's bodyguard. Carl would be the muscle and Victor had the connections. It seemed they would run the school now.

The day went by pretty smoothly. There was no trash-talking between the Conquistadors and Victor. Nothing came up. As Hernan, Cisco, and I walked home from school that afternoon I started to feel at ease. Nobody looked around for Victor because we all knew he took the bus home. Then I noticed something. Out of the corner of my eye I could see that Hernan was thinking about something. Cisco, too. I wished I had walked home with Henrietta instead of the guys. She was strolling a couple of blocks behind us with some of her girlfriends. Just as I thought about making a break for it and running back to them, it happened.

"Manny. You still friends with Carl?" Hernan asked.

I didn't really think we weren't friends anymore but I couldn't say that to the guys. Carl was a friend of Victor. Victor was an enemy of Hernan. Hernan was a Conquistador. I was a Conquistador. So that meant I couldn't be Victor's friend.

"Nah. Not really," I replied.

"How come?" Hernan asked.

"That's Victor's friend."

Hernan got bossy with me. "Well, you got to start being friends with him again."

"What?"

"You got to be his friend again. We need something."

"Like what?" I asked, not having a clue as to what we could want from Carl.

The tidal wave of trouble I had sensed was coming a crashed over me. "Some herb," Hernan answered.

"What? No way!"

Cisco spoke up. "Come on, man. You got to."

"We want like twenty dollars worth," Hernan said. "Tell him to put it on credit for you."

I felt like I had just swallowed a rock. That nauseous feeling I'd been getting since the Conquistadors first started returned. I didn't know what to think, what to say, or how to act.

"What do you want that for?" fell out of my mouth.

"To smoke it, fool!" Hernan said.

Hernan and Cisco began to laugh. Just then Bartolomeu, Nando, and Ferdinand ran up behind us on the sidewalk. They'd had after-school detention.

"What's up?" Bartolomeu asked.

"Manny's never smoked herb!" Cisco said.

"What?" Ferdinand began to laugh.

Soon they were all laughing at me.

"Manny never smokes 'cause he's a family man, remember? He's got his wife and their mortgage!"

The guys laughed their heads off. Then they started telling stories about the times they'd gotten high. I was still in shock over what they wanted me to do. I kept my mouth shut and tried to figure out a way to tell them that I couldn't do what they were asking me.

When we got to my block I felt a sense of both relief and dread. The good thing was that I could be away from the Conquistadors and what they were asking me to do. The bad thing was that after I walked away from them I'd be alone with my problems.

"So you're gonna take care of that thing for us, right?" Hernan asked.

All the guys were watching, so I couldn't hem and haw.

"Yeah," I said right back to him.

"That's my homeboy!" Hernan said, giving me a bro-shake.

"Twenty dollars worth!" Cisco added, so I wouldn't forget.

"Right," I replied.

As I turned away from them to walk down my block, it seemed like I was entering a black hole.

Chapter 8

ONE TIME IN SCIENCE CLASS our teacher had told us about black holes. Their gravity is so strong that they suck up everything into them, even light. And once something goes in, it can never come back out. It just disappears into that abyss. Our universe has black holes, somewhere out there. And now Orbe Nuevo had one. It was called the Conquistadors, and I was the one being sucked into it.

I felt like I needed a doctor, somebody to tell me just exactly why I said I would make a drug deal for the guys. That's what it was, straight up. No matter how I tried to make it sound nice, or like a favor, or like friends needing help with something, it was nothing more than a regular old illegal drug deal.

When I got home that Monday afternoon, the last thing I wanted was to run into my abuela. I yelled out hi and went straight up to my room. I wanted to close the door, hop into bed, and hide under the covers. But if I did that and wasn't sick, my abuela would think I'd gone *loco*, so I turned on my gamebox instead. For a long time I just stared at the TV screen. I couldn't play the game. My mind was still on the whole conversation about the herb.

I didn't want to think about the guys getting mixed up with drugs. Everything I'd heard about drugs for as long as I could remember was bad. On the TV shows and in the movies, all you ever saw was something bad happening whenever drugs were involved. People got sick. They got hurt. They went to jail, like Vasco. Now here I was about to get mixed up in all of that.

To try and take my mind off of things, I reached into my backpack and grabbed the book I'd checked out from the library. I climbed up on my bed and started to read. It was a good story. A guy was going to drive across America with his dog. He had to get all his stuff together for the trip. That's what I wanted to do, to get away and go on a trip somewhere. If I weren't twelve, I'd just pack up everything and take off. Maybe I'd go to the other side of the country, like to Maine. They fished there. I could get a job fishing and just disappear. I'd be Manny the fisherman. I wouldn't tell anybody where I was from or that I was a Conquistador, or that I had a friend named Carl who sold drugs in the seventh grade, or that I bought some for my friends who became sick on them.

The guy in the book I was reading lived on Long Island, New York. I remembered that place from another story I'd read last summer. The story was about a guy who knew this crazy rich guy. That was another place I could go to disappear. I didn't understand a lot of the story, but Long Island sounded like a nice place to hide. The guy's name in that story was Gatsby. I could be him. I'd be Manny Gatsby, eccentric millionaire in love with a crazy lady named Daisy. I could throw big parties and nobody would know who I was. The only part I didn't like about that fantasy was getting killed in my pool.

"Manny, what's wrong?" I heard from out of nowhere.

I looked up. My abuela was standing in the doorway. I must've read and daydreamed for a long time, because it was seven-thirty already and I hadn't gone down for dinner yet.

"Huh?" I replied.

"Are you sick?"

"No. I was just reading. It's a really good book."

"Come and eat. It's getting late."

As I ate I tried to figure out a way to get out of making the deal for the guys. Maybe if I pretended to be sick, I could stay home for a couple of days, I thought. That would buy me some time. The guys might make the deal for themselves while I was out of school. But if I came down with something, my abuela would make me go see a doctor. And if I went to the doctor, he'd know real fast that there was nothing wrong with me.

I finished my dinner, then went to my room to do my homework. But I couldn't focus. Two choices kept crossing my mind. Tell the guys no and lose my friends. Or do the deal and keep my friends. I had to do the deal, I decided.

Making the decision took away some stress. After a little while I was actually able to do my homework. I didn't feel like gaming, so I got dressed for sleep and climbed into bed.

I had to come up with a plan on how to make the deal with Carl. I hadn't even talked to him in the last couple of months. Carl's a good guy, I reminded myself. I just had to catch him where we could talk business in private. There was no way I was going to risk letting other kids overhear.

The next day at school I had nothing else on my mind. From the time I got there in the morning I was on the lookout for Carl. As I sat at the lunch tables with the rest of the Conquistadors before first period, I saw him standing in his usual spot with

Victor across the quad. There were a few girls standing around them and they were being all goofy. Funny how guys act different when girls are around. I wondered if I acted different when Henrietta was around.

"Manny. You got that thing covered?" Hernan asked me.

I turned toward him and nodded. I was afraid to even talk about it. If I didn't say anything about it, it almost seemed like it wasn't real, like I wasn't just about to make a drug deal for my friends. Words somehow made things more official. I guess because you can't take them back.

It wasn't until PE that I found a chance to talk to Carl. We were on the soccer field, about halfway through the game. Carl was playing goalie because he's so big. And I was playing defense because I was playing so lousy that day. Even the coach noticed that I wasn't all there. He sent me back from striker to defense.

Our team was doing well. The ball was all the way at the other end of the field for most of the game. That's when I got the chance to talk to Carl. We were both back by the goal. I asked him if he'd played any new games.

"Carjack!" he replied.

"Me too. I got it for Christmas. My abuela gave it to me."

"Which one did you get?"

"All three."

Carl didn't act like he was holding a grudge against anybody. We talked like we'd talked before the Conquistadors got started. He wanted to borrow one of my games and I said that was cool. When we had about ten minutes left of PE I decided it was time to ask him. I felt so stupid, like I was weak because I couldn't say no to Hernan and the Conquistadors.

As we were watching the play downfield, I sprang the deal on him.

"Yo, *ese?*"

"Yeah?"

"You still selling?"

"Yeah, why?"

"Can you hook me up with twenty dollars worth?"

"You got the cash?"

"No. On credit."

"Credit! Shhh. I guess. When you gonna pay me?"

"You'll get it."

"Loan me two Carjack games and I'll hold them for security. Be at the gates after school. Don't tell nobody I gave you credit, fool!"

"Cool."

That part was done. I felt a sense of relief. When the bell rang, I changed my clothes in the locker room and went to lunch. Part of me felt good knowing that Carl and I were still friends. But the rest of me just felt bad 'cause I'd gotten myself mixed up in something that I didn't want to be mixed up in.

By science class at the end of the day, I was a nervous wreck. I was just minutes from following through on something illegal, something I didn't want to do. I must have a more expressive face than anybody around. People always know when something is on my mind. My math teacher must've noticed something was odd, and he asked me if I was all right. I nodded.

The bell rang. I grabbed my book bag and tried to act normal though inside my heart was racing. I thought about going to the bathroom and just staying there until everyone had gone home. Just get it over with, I told myself, and started walking to the gates.

I could see Carl standing there. He had his backpack and sweatshirt slung over his shoulder. He was reading a book.

Here I am going nuts, and he's standing there reading a book, I thought. I could see the guys waiting for me a little ways down the street. Why couldn't one of them be doing this?

When I got to where Carl was standing, he looked up. He raised his hand to give me a bro-shake so I stuck my hand out in the air. When our hands made contact, I felt something slide in between them. It felt like a wad of plastic.

"Peace out, Manny. I'll catch you later," Carl said, walking off.

The wad of plastic was still in my hand. I nervously wondered if anyone was watching. I tried to be cool but I fumbled with the wad. I shoved it into my pocket and started over to the guys, who were acting goofy. They hadn't even gotten high yet and they were already acting stupid, I thought. What do they need the herb for?

When I reached them, we started down the street together. Henrietta was waiting for me a little ways up the block. She was by herself and looked annoyed at having to wait for me. Before she could say anything, Hernan spoke up.

"Sorry, girl. Your man's gotta talk business with the guys," he said.

I couldn't say anything. The guys were there. So I just kept walking on and left her standing alone.

We continued down the street. Cop cars were passing us like they usually did after school. I could go to jail, I thought. I was a twelve-year-old criminal. Unlike me, the guys didn't seem stressed. They were clowning and horse-playing like usual.

We approached my block. A few more steps and I'd be free, I thought with relief. I could hand them the herb, go home, and forget the whole thing.

We stopped at the corner. I reached into my pocket and palmed the little wad of plastic.

"Okay guys. Peace out," I said, sticking out my hand for a bro-shake with Hernan.

He did the same, and when our hands made contact I passed the little wad of plastic to Hernan, the same way Carl had done to me. Hernan seemed to know what he was doing. He didn't fumble with the wad like I had. He took it and coolly slipped his hand in his pocket. It was done.

"You're not coming with us?" Hernan asked.

"No, I've got to do homework."

"Come on, man. It's fun."

"Nah, I can't do it. I'll see you guys. *Mañana*," I said, turning around and heading home.

When I got home, I felt so good, I started eating all kinds of snacks. My abuela wondered what was up, so I told her I had had a test that day and hadn't had time for lunch. I thought it made more sense to tell her that, rather than that I had had to make an illegal drug deal for the guys and was so worried that I couldn't eat.

I'd gamed in my room for about an hour when my abuela came up with the phone.

"Mannnny. It's your girrrrllfriend!" she said, giggling.

I slapped my hand to my forehead as I remembered I'd given her the cold shoulder on the way home from school. She's probably mad at me, I thought, taking the phone.

"What's wrong with you?" Henrietta blurted out.

"Nothing."

"How come you didn't even say anything to me?"

"I was with the guys, and we had to take care of something."

"That's still no reason why you couldn't say hi or bye."

I apologized to Henrietta as best I could. I didn't want to hurt her feelings. But though she was my girlfriend, I couldn't tell her the truth about what was going on.

After a while Henrietta started to sound like her usual self. She talked about all kinds of things—school, friends, and music. I started gaming again like I usually did when she started talking a lot. When her mom called her to help for dinner, we said bye.

I decided to do my homework. I was much more focused, now that I felt like things were going to be all right. I finished up my homework around ten, then gamed some more, then went to bed, hoping for the best. I hoped that the guys wouldn't get into trouble with that herb I'd bought for them. I hoped things would settle down for me at school.

For the rest of the school week, things went by smoothly. My focus was back so my grades were good. The guys were happy 'cause I'd bought them the herb. Henrietta was walking home with me again. Then Friday afternoon came along, and things got weird. Well, not really weird, but different.

As Henrietta and I strolled home from school with the guys a little ahead of us I noticed the they were really excited. During the last couple of periods of school, they'd been talking about hanging out that night. Their code name for the herb was Juanita. I heard them talking all afternoon about how they were going to see Juanita that night, and how cool it was going to be. Henrietta heard them throwing Juanita's name around, too, and asked who she was. I told her the guys were just being goofy.

The guys had found a new spot to hang out, a cul de sac in a housing development. The recession had shut the project down so now there were just a bunch of half-made houses. They liked to go there because there were no grown-ups around. Usually they'd just take some cigarettes, smoke, listen to music, and clown each other. But now they had Juanita.

There was no way I was going with them. I didn't care if they thought I was a wimp or a girly-man or anything. I'd tell them anything, but I wasn't going. Then I turned to Henrietta, and the words popped out.

"So you wanna come over and watch TV tonight?"

I couldn't believe I'd said it. I'd never asked a girl over in my life. Was I crazy? I was so surprised, I hardly heard Henrietta say yeah.

"Huh?" I said, out of habit.

"Yeah, I'll come over. What time?"

"Seven," I answered.

"Cool."

We got to her block and she stopped to give me a kiss on the cheek like always. We said bye and I walked on with the guys.

"How long you been married, Manny?" Cisco joked.

I let the guys tease me. I didn't care. Henrietta was less trouble than they were. And, I felt kind of guilty thinking it, but she was also the perfect alibi.

The guys still tried to get me to go with them. They begged, but I stayed firm. I was having company over. It felt kind of cool to tell them that, like I was a grown-up or something. Best of all, it worked. They laid off laying on the guilt.

I got home and told my abuela that Henrietta was coming over.

"What?" she said, with a big smile. "Really! A date! My little Manny's having a date over?"

I felt about three years old. Nobody can make you feel more like a baby than your grandma.

My abuela quickly started to plan.

"I'm going to make popcorn. And I'll order a pizza. We have soda. You can watch a movie."

"Okay, Nana." I left her to her planning and made my way upstairs.

I wasn't too worried about having Henrietta over. To me, she was just another friend—but a girl, one who liked to kiss me on the cheek. On TV they make it seem like relationships are always so crazy and bad. To me, it didn't feel like that. Maybe I wasn't really in love with her. Maybe it was only love when it got crazy and bad. Either way, she was a great excuse to not hang out with the guys.

I gamed till six forty-five, then I stopped to get ready. I wasn't going to make a big deal about Henrietta coming over, even if my abuela was. All I did was wash up and put on a clean shirt. While I was washing up, I heard the doorbell ring and the pizza man drop off a pizza. I could also smell popcorn being made downstairs. My abuela was having a heyday with this, I thought.

I got downstairs at seven and noticed my abuela had straightened everything up to look extra nice. The cushions on the couches were all straight. The carpet was clean, with those little track marks on them that made you know they were just vacuumed. I could smell air freshener in the air. My abuela had done everything.

In the kitchen there were some two-liter bottles of soda on the counter, an extra large pizza with pepperoni, and a huge bowl of popcorn—with more popping on the stove. My abuela made popcorn the old-fashioned way, in a pot instead of the microwave. She said it tasted better that way. It looked like enough food to feed ten people, not just two kids.

"Dang, Nana!" I said. "You didn't need to do all this."

"Hey. Watch your mouth!" she scolded. She then smiled and said, "I don't know. Maybe you two will be hungry. Yeah, maybe I got a little carried away."

A little after seven the doorbell rang and my abuela answered. Standing at the door was Henrietta and her mom, holding her baby sister. Henrietta wasn't dressed up or anything but her hair was pulled back tight in a bun like it was for the Christmas party. Her mom had a big smile on her face, like my abuela. I guessed that they thought it was cute that Henrietta and I were going to watch TV together. They all came in and Henrietta's mom found a seat in the kitchen with the baby. She and my abuela started talking. They spoke Spanish so fast that I could hardly understand them. Henrietta came into the family room and sat down on the couch. I showed her the movies we had, and she picked out *Raiders of the Lost Ark*. It was my favorite, so I felt relieved we weren't going to watch something boring. I put in the movie and sat down on the couch with her. She was being all quiet. I guess she was a little nervous like me. If it were the guys who were over, we'd be clowning around and hitting each other and stuff. But I didn't feel that was the way you acted with friends who were girls.

I'd seen the movie many times before, but it was still exciting. I didn't even notice that Henrietta's mom and baby sister had left until my abuela brought us some pizza and soda. Henrietta ate three pieces of pizza and she smiled a lot, so I guess she was having a good time.

We didn't talk much at all. We just watched the movie and ate. I didn't feel like talking anyway. The only real story I had was what had happened that week with the herb and the guys, and I couldn't share that with her.

I felt nice being at home. I wondered what the guys were doing. They were probably high and acting stupid and about to get caught. I just wanted to be Manny. I thought about how it was that, as you grow up, it got harder and harder to just be you. If it kept going on like this, who would I be when I was a grown-up? I couldn't dress the way I wanted to, or have the friends that I wanted to have. I'd be doing things that I didn't want to do for people, just to keep them as my friends.

The movie was over at about ten. Henrietta's mom hadn't come to pick her up yet. Of all things we started playing rock-paper-scissors while we waited for her. I thought it was kind of kiddish, but once we got started it was a lot of fun. We broke even for eight rounds of the game, then I beat her in tiebreaker.

The doorbell rang and we got up. My abuela answered the door again. Henrietta's mom was standing at the door with the baby, just like when they had arrived. The baby was asleep, so my abuela whispered hi and handed Henrietta's mom a bag of pop-corn, some pizza wrapped up in plastic, and a two-liter bottle of soda to take home. Right before Henrietta left she kissed me on the cheek.

My abuela and Henrietta's mom had big smiles on their faces and said, "Awww," like they'd just seen a cute puppy or something.

I felt three years old again, but I smiled and said bye. After they left I helped my abuela put away the food.

"I think she had a good time, Romeo!" my abuela said, wearing a big grin on her face.

"It was all right."

"Ah. Listen to Don Juan now! You be nice to her, Manny. Women have memories like elephants. If you're not nice to them, it will come back to you. Remember what I said."

I nodded and went upstairs. I thought about what my abuela had said. I'd learned that lesson a long time ago. That's why I tried to be nice to everyone—well, everyone that the Conquistadors allowed me to be nice to anyways.

The next morning I was up early. I smelled breakfast cooking. The sun was out. It was Saturday and I could play all day. My abuela had breakfast all spread out on the table, like we were having company.

"Morning. What's up with the table?"

"Nothing. Just thought it would be nice."

Breakfast was good. My abuela had made chorizo and eggs. There was a pitcher of orange juice, too. When I finished, I felt stuffed. I was feeling sleepy, too, like I could go back to bed. Then my abuela started acting strange, like she was plotting something.

"So you had a big breakfast?" she asked.

"Yeah."

"And it is Saturday so you have nothing to do all day but what you want to do, right?"

"Yeah."

"Not a care in the world, huh?"

At this point I knew my abuela wanted me to do something for her and was trying to make me feel guilty so I would agree to do it.

"Yeah. What do you want me to do?"

"Who said I want you to do anything?"

My abuela was too good at this game. I couldn't win, so I just waited. Like nothing was on her mind, she started scrubbing the dishes. It must have been almost a whole minute before she started with, "I wonder what it would feel like to be a new kid in town and not know anybody? I'd probably just hang around my house all weekend long, not talking to a single person. If I was lucky, I might have a kid who lived next door to me, or across the street even, who was about my age. Then I'd have a built-in friend close to home."

"Maybe," I said, not getting it yet.

"Was your breakfast good?"

"Yeah."

"Better than having cereal this morning, huh?"

"Yeah. What do you want me to do, Nana?"

"A favor."

"What?"

"Go look out the window in the front room."

I got up and went to the front room. I pulled the blinds and looked outside. I didn't see anything unusual at first. Then I saw a black kid about my age across the street, playing on a skateboard in the neighbor's driveway.

My abuela had followed me into the front room. "His name is Bernard. He and his mom just moved," she said.

"Is he going to my school?"

"Catholic school."

Bernard had a strange beanie on his head. It was colorful and had two drawstrings on it that dangled down. It looked like a hippie beanie.

"Is he a hippie?" I asked my abuela seriously.

My abuela chuckled. "Maybe he is. Go over and introduce yourself. See what he's up to. Maybe you two have things in common."

I didn't mind the idea of being nice, but the whole idea of being forced to be friends bothered me. Still, there was no way I couldn't do as my abuela asked.

"He's a skater," I said.

"And you have a new skateboard from Christmas that you haven't even ridden," she reminded me. "Think about all you have, Manny. Are you so happy and content that you can't have another friend?"

That hit home. My abuela had no idea that I was wondering why I was friends with the friends I had.

I went upstairs, grabbed my skateboard, and went outside. Bernard was concentrating real hard on some tricks he was doing on his board, so he didn't notice me at first. I stood watching him for a while. He fell trying to do a 360, then caught a glimpse of me.

"What's up, man?" he said.

"Hey," I replied. "I'm Manny."

"I'm Bernard. You ride?" he asked, pointing at my skateboard.

"Not really. Just got it. Never been on one."

"Well, let's go!" Bernard said. He hopped on his board and took off down the street.

Not sure what to do, I threw my board down like him, and jumped on, but fell flat on my back as the board slipped out from under my feet. Bernard didn't see it. But as my eyes scanned around the neighborhood, I saw my abuela peeking out the window of our house, laughing her head off.

I got up, dusted myself off, put the board in place, and placed one foot firmly on top to test how slippery it was. Then I kicked off, and I was moving. Looking ahead, I saw Bernard all the way at the corner of our block. He was zigzagging, spinning around, and doing tricks on the curb. He looked back and waited for me. Slowly I made my way to him, one kick at a time.

"You're doing good, man. Keep it up!" he said. Then he was off again, zooming down the street.

Bernard could direct the board with his feet, but I had to bend down to guide it with my hands. Once I did, I planted one foot on and pushed off with the other to follow him. As I struggled to stay on the board, I wondered if any of the Conquistadors were watching. They'd think I'd gone *loco*. Here I was, barely able to stay up on a skateboard, skating my hardest to follow some kid with a hippie beanie on. It even sounded funny to me. As I smiled at the thought, I realized I was having fun.

Bernard and I skated all over our neighborhood. We even skated into other people's neighborhoods. I learned it was a good way to get around. What might take a half hour to walk only took a few minutes on a skateboard. I was sweating and struggling to keep up with Bernard but he'd always stop and wait for me if I fell too far behind. After a couple hours I could ride pretty good on it. I couldn't do any of the tricks that Bernard could do, but I was able to stay fairly close to him when we were on a straightaway. At the park near my school, we took a break and sat on some picnic tables.

Bernard told me that he and his mom were from up north and that they'd just moved here. His mom worked as a nurse and had a real busy schedule. He only got to see her on some weekends and a couple of hours each night. He didn't know much about his dad. He was some guy his mom had known in college. I told him about my parents, who were down in Mexico, and my abuela here. He asked me about my school and if it was cool. I told him yeah, and I asked him about his school. He said it was all right but that he had to wear a uniform every day. After our break, we took off again. I wished I had a mile counter on my skateboard because it seemed like we rode for a lot of miles.

We finally got back to our block. I wondered how long we'd ridden for. There would be no soccer this afternoon, I thought. I was too tired to do anything. As soon as I walked inside the house, my abuela popped up. She had a big grin on her face.

"I hate to say it, Manny, but I told you so!" She started laughing at me.

"Whatever," I replied, trying not to laugh. I went straight to the kitchen for lunch. My grandma was always right in the end.

I grabbed two pieces of leftover pizza from my date with Henrietta and went up to my room. I was so sleepy that all I wanted to do was take a nap. As soon as I finished eating, I dozed off. I didn't wake up until seven-thirty, and I was more sore than I'd ever been in my life. Even my skin seemed to hurt. Skateboarding was a tough sport, I realized. My abuela must've known I was going to ache because she was there with some aspirin when I woke up.

"Skateboarding isn't for wimps, is it?" my abuela said with a smile.

"Yeah," I said, then dozed back off.

Sunday morning came on me like a surprise. I woke up and the morning sun was shining. I was still in the clothes I'd worn to go skateboarding with Bernard. My abuela must've put some blankets on me while I was sleeping because I was all tucked in.

"Manny!" I heard her call from downstairs. "Get ready for church. I don't want to be late."

I felt a little better than I had the night before, but still sore. It took me some time to get out of bed and move normally. I took a bath and got ready for church. As I came down the stairs, the doorbell rang.

"I'll get it," I called out.

I opened the door. There, standing in a really cool suit, was Bernard.

"Hey, what's up, man?" he said.

"Hey, what's up?" I said back.

"I'm going to church with you guys."

"Oh," I said. "Come in."

Later on I learned that Bernard's mom had talked to my

abuela about taking Bernard with us. She had to work but she wanted him to go to church just the same. Bernard had cereal with me, then we all went to church together. Bernard must've really liked that colorful beanie because he even wore it into church. A few people stared, but nobody said anything. Another really neat thing that happened on account of Bernard was that we got to stop for hamburgers on the way home. My abuela and I never did that. As we sat in the restaurant eating, I felt a little guilty that I'd had to be conned into being Bernard's friend. It was turning out to be pretty cool. He wasn't bossy. He wasn't getting me to make drug deals for him. He was being a pretty cool friend.

That made me think about the guys and how they had gone out Friday night. I wondered if everything had turned out all right. I hoped that they hadn't gotten hurt or in trouble. I was lucky, I thought. I got to be myself, Manny, all weekend long. But tomorrow was Monday. I'd be back in school and a Conquistador all over again.

Chapter 9

THE LAST THING I EXPECTED to hear from the guys on Monday morning was, "Manny, you gotta get us some more herb."

I couldn't believe it. All the agony I had gone through the week before for that stuff, and they wanted me to do it all over again.

"What?" I asked.

Hernan repeated, "You gotta get us some more herb."

This time I had the sense to say, "No way. I didn't even party with you guys. There he is." I pointed to Carl, who was standing in his usual spot across the quad. "Go make your own deal."

"Check it out, man. Carl is still burning over that Victor thing," Hernan replied. "He won't hook us up."

"I don't want to get mixed up in it anymore."

"Come on, man! It's Conquistadors business," Nando said.

Bartolomeu was standing nearby. He had a serious look on his face. He stared at me for a few seconds, then said, "Maybe he doesn't want to be a Conquistador anymore."

I couldn't believe he actually said what I'd been thinking.

"Shut up, man!" Hernan said. "This is my homeboy. We've been friends since kindergarten. He's an original Conquistador."

Hernan stuck up for me. Right then, that's all I could think of, that he stuck up for me. He was right. We'd been friends since kindergarten. I couldn't turn my back on that.

"All right," I said. "I'll get it. Where's the money?"

Big smiles broke across the Conquistador's faces.

"Credit, *ése!*" Cisco said, and they all broke out laughing.

I shook my head. Things were quickly going from bad to worse. Where were the guys going to come up with money to pay for the herb they were buying? This wasn't like elementary school, when you borrowed a dollar for lunch from somebody and didn't pay it back. This was a lot of money. They'd be in the hole for forty dollars to Carl. Carl saw himself as a businessman. He wouldn't just forget the money. If they didn't pay him back, he'd do something. And now that Victor was a member of Playaz, I didn't want to think about what that something could be. Every instinct I had was telling me this was a bad idea, but I went along because I didn't know what else to do.

It wasn't that hard to make the deal this time. I did it the same way: I spoke to Carl during PE and set up the deal. He met me at the gates again after school. He gave me some trouble over the credit thing, but then he caved. He said he'd hold two more of my video games as collateral for the herb. I didn't mind because I'd played them both out. So the guys met me on the curb after school just like the time before, and we all walked home together, with Henrietta trailing behind.

That was the beginning. The drug deal became a weekly thing. The guys would make the request, and I would make the deal. Carl started considering me one of his regular customers, except that all my deals were on credit. When the tab got to eighty dollars he wanted to cut me off. I offered him a couple more of my games as security and told him not to sweat it, that the guys were good for it. Carl said something that I'll never forget. Henrietta had said it before, too. After agreeing to give me more credit, Carl turned to me and said, "Be careful, Manny. Those guys are going to get you in trouble."

What a thing to hear from your drug dealer, I thought. But Carl was right. Henrietta was right. Even I was right, but there was nothing I could do about it. They were my friends.

I didn't want to think of my friends as drug addicts, but in reality that's what they were becoming. Herb became the only thing they talked about. Where could they get some? Where could they smoke some? What could they do when they smoked it? They also started to think everybody was a narc, or a rat. Whenever someone would come around that wasn't a Conquistador, they'd shush up and stop talking. If a teacher walked by, they would do the same thing. Once the teacher passed, they would just break out laughing like it was the funniest thing in the world to almost get caught talking about smoking herb. They were becoming regular old druggies.

Even their jokes now were all about herb, or Juanita, or about being high. I just tuned them out. Hearing them talk was like hearing someone tell the same bad joke over and over again.

The cul de sac had become the new regular hangout for the guys. They started ditching classes and going there to hide out. They'd spend late nights there listening to music and ditching their parents. They went there every day after school. I never went with them, but they'd tell me everything they did there. Of course they got high. I didn't really want to hear about it. I didn't want to end up like my abuela's son. And I didn't want them to either.

I'd known what herb smelled like for years. Vasco had always had that smell. I lived in his room now, and when I opened his drawers I could still smell it. Sometimes when I was in the backyard playing, I would smell herb coming from the neighbor's backyard. A young couple lived there, and when they had friends over, I would always smell it. When my abuela smelled it, too, she'd come out to our backyard and bring me in.

"Manny, enough playing outside. Come inside," she'd say in a serious tone.

And now every time I saw the guys, they smelled like that smell.

They were acting stupider than normal. The last week of March, Hernan caught a week-long home suspension for laughing. I wasn't in class with him at the time, but I heard about it later. The story went like this. He goes into English Support class and sits down. The teacher calls his name for attendance and he just starts laughing. He won't stop. The teacher warns him three times before writing him up and sending him out. Then he gets to the principal's office and does the same thing. He can't even hear the principal telling him that he's being put on home suspension, because he's laughing so hard. Now that, to me, is just plain stupid.

Cisco was getting busted for doing dumb things, too. One time he showed up to PE and started doing his jumping jacks with the rest of his class, then out of his pockets dropped four or five tagging markers. Because they're banned at school, he picked up three days of home suspension plus two days of clean-up detention.

It didn't stop there, though. Ferdinand picked up a couple of days for open-hand hitting a girl on the face. Bartolomeu picked up three days for bullying. Nando was the only one who managed not to get caught. That didn't mean he wasn't doing stupid things, just that he was quiet enough and smart enough not to get caught.

It was as if they didn't care anymore about anything. Ferdinand and Nando had really strict parents, so they had to make *some* effort with school. But when it came to Hernan, Cisco, and Bartolomeu, they'd just given up flat. They were on academic detention every week and make-up tutoring every day. They were on discipline probation in every way. I lost count of all the school contracts they had to sign just to stay in school.

The weeks went by quickly. I tried to make the best of school and stay positive during the week, and I hung out with Henrietta or Bernard on the weekends. Henrietta liked coming over and watching movies, so we did that a lot. And Bernard and I went everywhere on skateboards. I was starting to get pretty good on my board. I could do 360s and nose slides. I could cut an empty swimming pool pretty good, too, but I couldn't go vertical yet. Bernard told me not to worry—it would come with practice. "Kids who try to go vertical before their time always end up with broken arms," he said.

Bernard was a very spiritual guy. I'd never known any kid quite like him. He was always talking about being at peace with yourself and others. He would talk about not forcing anything, because if you did, that was being at conflict with nature. When he'd talk about stuff like that, it would always make me think of Hernan and how he seemed to be in conflict with everybody and everything. I couldn't follow everything Bernard said, but I tried. Cool wasn't just an empty word when it came to Bernard, because he really was just that—cool. One day after I'd known him for a while, I noticed that he was wearing these geeky glasses. I thought they were new so I asked him about them, and he said he'd worn them all along and I just hadn't noticed. Now that's cool, I thought. When a person wears geeky glasses and you don't notice, that person has to be cool.

Bernard wanted to be psychologist. I'd never known what that really was until he explained it to me. The way he explained it, a psychologist helps people get over their problems. Not like medical problems that you see a doctor for, but like head problems when you have fears. That part I could relate to. I thought I would need one with all the stress the Conquistadors were putting me through.

Because the guys were always in trouble, Henrietta and I walked home from school together almost every day. Sometimes we'd hold hands. The first couple of times I was nervous, but then it became so regular I hardly even noticed. She'd tell me about how she saw me riding around with Bernard. She thought he was cool and crazy at the same time, especially with that beanie he wore. She'd tell me about the funny things her baby sister did and the crazy things her pop did. Now that the guys were getting high all the time, everybody at school knew, so she'd warn me not to hang around with them or I would end up getting busted right along with them. One time she asked me what I wanted to be when I grew up. I'd never really thought about it much. I'd had the usual kid dreams to be a professional soccer player, or a marine, but the word "archaeologist" popped out of my mouth.

"What? Me too!" she shrieked.

Then we both laughed because we had the same dream.

In the weeks leading up to spring break I thought a lot about breaking up with the Conquistadors. I figured I could just tell them that I was trying to get into a good college some day and I wanted to keep my nose clean. Some of them might even take it okay, like Ferdinand and Nando, and maybe Bartolomeu, too, but I figured Hernan and Cisco would be hurt. We were like brothers. All I had to do was look at them and I would see the kids they'd been in kindergarten, the first day even. We had been scared and didn't know anything. We shared a worktable then, and used the same glue, crayons, and everything. They were my first friends. Even now, sometimes I wondered if I should be like them and get high, too, and not care about school. It would be easier that way. But then I would think about all the things I wanted to do, like being an archaeologist and having a family. And the fact of the matter was that I *liked* learning new things in school and keeping my head straight. I liked making my abuela and parents happy. It's a horrible feeling to know that I've made them sad.

Every now and then I would see Hernan's mom or Cisco's parents coming to school to pick them up when they were in trouble. Hernan's mom would have this hurt look on her face, like the world was falling apart. Cisco's mom and dad always looked tired, like they'd been through it a thousand times. I guess they had, with all the trouble that Cisco's brothers used to get into.

The next time I'd see Hernan or Cisco after they'd come back from a suspension they would act like it was the coolest thing in the world. They'd laugh and joke like they had it all under control. To them, a suspension was a vacation. They stayed with their *tíos* or *tías* and gamed all day. Or they went to the cul de sac and got high. When I'd be at school all day not seeing them, sometimes I'd get sad thinking about them sitting at the cul de sac by themselves, getting high just to pass the time. To me that would be miserable. I wouldn't get to go to social studies, which I loved. I'd miss the library, and my teachers, and my other friends like Nicky. I wouldn't get to see Henrietta. I'd be nowhere.

Something else was bugging me too. The guys were in debt pretty deep to Carl. They owed a hundred and forty dollars. Carl was starting to get real annoyed with me. He had eight of my games in collateral for the herb, but that wasn't enough. Now on Mondays, when he knew I was going to ask him for some herb for the guys, he would say he didn't have any herb and that we'd better pay up what we owed or stuff was going to happen. Carl knew I wasn't into herb, and he realized it was for the guys.

"Look, Manny. I know it's probably hard for them to come up with all the money, but how about half? If I had half, I'd feel better about this credit thing. I don't give anybody credit but you, and I think I've made a mistake," Carl told me.

"You'll get your money," I promised.

"When?"

"Come on. We're not going anywhere. It's us, the guys."

"No. It's *those* guys, Manny. And I'm getting tired of this. I pay for it! It costs me money!"

"I know. You'll get it."

Carl would shake his head in disbelief and walk away. But he'd always be there at the gates after school.

Victor was starting to get involved, too. He was always near Carl when I tried to make a deal for the guys. He'd give me this look like I better not think of trying to ditch out on paying Carl. Ever since joining the Playaz, he had developed this hard look. I rarely saw him smile nowadays. Sometimes I would look at him and his eyes were lifeless. I wondered what being in the Playaz was doing to him. What was he was doing and seeing that would take away the life in him? A few of us knew Victor's parents were drunks. It was stuff nobody talked about in school, unless they wanted to be mean. I knew where he lived. There were these apartments near the North side that were really run down.

Bernard and I skated through that area of town every now and then. We never stopped there. Once in a while there'd be crime scene yellow tape around a unit. There'd be broken bottles and empty cans lying around the street like there'd been a big party there—but there hadn't. It was like that all the time.

When I first met Victor he was the class clown. Sometimes he was so funny that even the teacher would laugh. He was the type of kid who could cut up in class and not get into trouble, because he made the class fun. He had so much happy energy around him, lively energy. If Bernard had known Victor he would have said that he had a positive life force. But that seemed to be leaving him. Now it seemed like he had a negative life force. His eyes were dark and cold. Everything was serious and intense. My abuela had pictures of her real family up on the walls in the front room. She had some of Vasco there too. When Vasco was young, he had a sparkle in his eyes and a big smile on his face. But in the older pictures, the sparkle and smile are gone. That's what was happening to Victor. He was getting Vasco's eyes.

The Playaz had never touched my life before Victor joined them. They were just a gang that people would mention in passing, almost like a myth. I saw stories about them in the papers and on the TV. Sometimes when there was a shooting, the suspects would be members of the Playaz. Or there was a big drug bust, and some Playaz would be caught, like when Vasco got arrested. I always wondered what guys got out of being in gangs. I knew from the Conquistadors that at times it felt neat to be in a club, but weren't we friends anyway before the gang?

I felt guilty about it, but a part of me hoped that the Playaz would notice Hernan and Cisco and decide they wanted them. Sometimes I imagined that they would be jumped into the Playaz and eventually forget this whole Conquistadors gang.

If they felt part of the big time, they would be happy and I could quietly fade out of the gang picture altogether. In the back of my mind I knew that the Playaz probably wouldn't take Hernan and Cisco. They were too goofy. And now that they were smoking herb all the time, they were sloppy and goofy. The Playaz, a serious outfit, with a serious agenda, would never want that. But they did want Carl.

The Monday of the week before spring break the guys were shocked back into reality. Ten minutes before the start of school we were at our usual spot sitting on the lunch tables when I looked across the quad and saw the unbelievable. Carl was in his usual place, too, goofing with some loud girls. Sitting on top of his head was an orange cap. It made no sense to me, and yet it made perfect sense. Carl wasn't the type of guy who wanted to be in a gang. He liked to be in control, not taking orders from anybody. And the heart of Carl was pure geek. But Carl was a straight-up businessman, too, even if he was only in seventh grade. He had learned somewhere around fourth grade that if he bought ten candy bars for forty cents a piece, he could sell them to the kids at school for a dollar each. Then he moved on to chips. Now his product was herb. As I saw it, Carl wouldn't join the Playaz because he wanted to be a gangster. It was just good business, nothing more, nothing less.

I took a deep breath. The guys were probably stoned. They were clowning and hadn't noticed yet. I nudged Nando and nodded in Carl's direction.

"Check it out," Nando said to the others.

The rest of the guys looked in Carl's direction. They sobered night up. Nothing was said for a while.

"How much we owe that fool?" Hernan asked.

"One hundred and sixty," Ferdinand replied.

"I guess we better pay him," suggested Cisco.

"Shhh. *You* pay him!" Hernan said, with a tone in his voice like nothing in the world was going to make him pay Carl the money they owed.

I pretended not to hear, for no other reason than my own peace of mind. I told myself that Hernan was just kidding, that he was going to make good on the money he owed. I hoped the rest of the guys wouldn't repeat anything Hernan had said. I prayed they didn't agree with him.

"He said he'd take something like half. That would be cool for a while," I said, trying to smooth things over.

Hernan took control. "Don't sweat it. We'll take care of it."

I believed him. I wasn't going to worry about it or get all stressed out. It wasn't my problem anyway, I convinced myself. I was just the middleman.

The guys didn't ask for their usual pick-up of the herb that day. I didn't know if it was because Carl was now a member of the Playaz, or for a worse reason. I didn't want to believe that they were messing around with speed. I didn't want to believe that the guys were that stupid or that far gone.

My suspicions were growing though. I noticed the guys were up and lively all the time and wouldn't shut up for anything. They had tons of energy—they played games in PE harder and faster than anybody. They were fidgety all the time, always tapping their feet or their pencils. Then, at other times, they were oddly quiet. Not quiet like at peace, but they seemed like they were fully alert yet zoned out. I had heard something at lunch one day that made me wonder. I was busy eating and the guys were rambling on about something. I wasn't sure which one said it, but it was something about Juanita being too expensive, and Crystal being a cheap date.

Speed was nothing but bad news. Some nights I would stay up late to watch the real-life cop shows with my abuela. It seemed everybody on the show was out of control on speed. Tweakers had a certain look about them. They panhandled and looked obsessed. The ones I saw on the streets were skinny as rails and their faces were broken out bad. Some of them had missing teeth. If my abuela and I were in the car, she'd glance at them on the streets and make the sign of the cross. It was sad. And now the guys were playing with becoming like that.

As I waited for school to start that day, I began to see the future of the Conquistadors like a chess game in my head. I saw the moves ahead of time. Every outcome I could think of led to a checkmate on the Conquistadors. If they paid Carl the money, it would eventually become a checkmate. If they didn't pay Carl the money, it would eventually become a checkmate. If they were doing speed now, it was checkmate. If they were just smoking herb and that's all, it was still a checkmate.

It was like I was treading water in the middle of the ocean and spring break was this life raft bobbing around in the distance. I could take a break from Conquistadors, from Carl and from not knowing what to do. Hernan would be working with his uncle like he always did on vacations, so there would be no trouble. Bernard and I could skate. Henrietta and I could watch movies. I could game all day and night.

The same way time disappeared when you were waiting for something horrible to happen, time seemed to expand and grow when you were waiting for something good. Those five weekdays before spring break seemed to last an eternity. On Monday I was wishing it was Tuesday. When it was Tuesday, I couldn't wait till Wednesday and so on. My abuela mentioned she was going to take Henrietta, Bernard, and me to the big amusement park in Anaheim. That's all I needed to hear. The clock seemed to stop on Wednesday and just stay there. I was like a zombie going to and from my classes. Each period felt like a full day.

I'd hardly noticed that Hernan had his denim jacket slung over his shoulder at the beginning of Wednesday and through the first two periods. In English, right in the middle of my class, the fire alarm went off. As soon as it started to ring, the teacher got a phone call from the office. She looked surprised and shocked at the same time. Then she had us get under our desks like it was a disaster drill or something. Kids were laughing and joking and saying how there was a drive-by shooting going on or something. We'd practiced drills for all kinds of things like that so we knew what to do. If it had been a real drive-by shooting, the school would go into lockdown. We'd be stuck in the same class, locked in, until we got the all-clear call from the office. We'd never had that happen, but we'd heard of schools that had. Sometimes kids would be there until six or seven at night. I started to get nervous. What if I had to go to the bathroom? What if I got hungry? From under my desk I looked up to the windows that lined the ceiling, and then I saw it.

Just a wisp at first, but then I saw more. It was billowing, wafting, gray. Smoke. Uh-oh, I thought, smoke! There really *was* something going on. I couldn't believe it at first. I nodded for Ferdinand to look up and out the window. He looked, then turned back to me. He must've understood before I did that a Conquistador had something to do with it, because he rolled his eyes. That's when it hit me. It was Hernan. That's why he'd had that denim jacket slung over his shoulder. He'd hidden something in there, like those paint cans that night we'd gone to the wash. *He* had started some fire or something. This was it, I thought. This was major. We were all going down.

"Okay kids," the teacher said, trying not to show that she was scared. "We are now under lockdown, so everybody try to get comfortable under your desk. If you can do your work under there, do your work. If you can read, then read. If you just want to sit with your head down, fine. You can lie down if you want."

Each thing she added to the list of things we could do under our desks made it clear to me that we weren't going anywhere for a long time. I couldn't believe that Hernan would pull something like this so close to spring break. I took out a book and started to read. Eventually we heard sirens, a lot of them. I started tracking time by chapters in my book. I'd read three, and we were still there under our desks. Every fifteen minutes or so, the teacher would get a call from the office. You couldn't tell much from what she was saying, just a lot of "I sees" and "all rights." She did give us updates a couple of times. From what she knew, there'd been some incendiary devices set off, or smoke bombs. They went off, and the fire alarm was pressed. The classes that were in session were to stay in their rooms until the fire department said it was all clear. There was one small detail that made everything crystal clear to me. She said that because PE was being held out on the baseball diamond, they were allowed to exit from the back gate and go home early. I rolled my eyes when I heard that.

It made perfect sense. Hernan, Cisco, and Bartolomeu all had third period PE. They had plotted this out so they could get out early for the day and go to the cul de sac and get high. Somehow, some way, they set off the smoke bombs while they were on the diamond. And right now, while I was scrunched up under my desk, hungry, bored, and needing the bathroom, they were getting high and talking smack about how they'd pulled off the ultimate prank.

Time went by even more slowly. After a couple of hours I had to use the bathroom badly. Some kids had lunches and snacks in their backpacks, so they broke them out and shared. I got half a tuna sandwich that was too salty from one kid, half a juice box from Nando, and an apple nobody wanted. A couple of the kids had cell phones and made calls home to their parents. I took a turn on one and called my abuela. She said she knew I was fine. She was watching the whole thing on the news, and I should just sit tight until they let us go.

After a while the waiting was unbearable. I guess because of the smoke, they shut down all the AC too. It was hot and the air smelled bad in the classroom. I needed to breathe in some fresh air. I daydreamed that we were hostages, and some terrorists were keeping us there. The terrorists were Hernan, Cisco, and Bartolomeu. They had us all scared and wouldn't let us go. I guess I must've dozed off, because the next thing I knew, the classroom door was being flung open by the teacher, and kids were getting up from under their desks. Ferdinand must have fallen asleep, too, because he was groggy. I looked at the clock on the wall. It said four-thirty, an hour after school normally got out. What a rip-off.

I threw my backpack over my shoulder and stumbled out into the daylight. I'd never appreciated the way the air smelled in Orbe Nuevo more than I did that afternoon, smog and all. When I got to the gates there were fire trucks everywhere, police cars, too. There were even a couple of those satellite vans from the news, with reporters and everything. My abuela was waiting for me just outside the gates. She had her housedress on and her arms folded. She smiled. I guess she thought it was funny, or maybe she was happy to see me. Either way, I needed to use the bathroom. I was hungry, too. And I was glad to be going home.

After I'd had something to eat and rested a little at home, I wanted to go to the cul de sac to find the guys. I needed to ask them why they pulled such a stupid move. I told my abuela that I was going to get some fresh air since I'd been locked up all day.

I'd never really been to the cul de sac before, I remembered, as I started walking up the street. I'd seen it from a distance as Bernard and I rode around, but I was almost too embarrassed to stop there with him. What if my friends were there and they were high? Bernard would've thought I was all into that kind of stuff, too. Keeping friends separate was just a reality of seventh grade, I thought. It was the same thing like how I could talk to Carl but the guys couldn't. It made sense to me at the time.

It was a long walk to the cul de sac. I realized why the guys liked it so much. Nobody went there unless they had to. And since the construction was shut down nobody had to. It was pretty dark by the time I got there, but I could hear laughter and music. I could also smell that smell.

The guys kind of panicked when they saw someone walking up the block. Then they noticed it was me. I heard a lot of cursing, then they got real quiet.

"It's Manny!" I heard one of the guys say in surprise.

"Manny!" I heard Hernan shout out.

"Hey," I replied.

I couldn't see too well in the darkness, but Hernan, Cisco, and Bartolomeu were all sprawled out on the front porch of one of the partially finished model houses. I could hear a radio playing oldies. They all started laughing their heads off like crazy for some unknown reason. The guys still had on their clothes from PE.

I got to the point. "So what was that all about? We were locked in until four-thirty!"

The guys just started laughing harder.

Cisco spoke up. "Come on, man! We couldn't let too many people know."

"Yeah, man. We had to keep it a secret or it wouldn't have worked," Hernan said between chuckles.

"Do you know how much trouble you caused?" I asked. "The TV news came out. Bomb squad! Everything."

The guys hushed up and looked at me with wide eyes.

"No way!" said Bartolomeu.

"Really. Fire trucks. Police. Everybody was there," I said angrily.

The guys seemed scared for a moment.

"Did anybody say anything about us?" Hernan asked, growing graver.

"Not that I know of," I replied.

"Oh. Then it's cool!" Hernan said. He started chuckling again.

Soon the other guys were laughing, too. They were high. It didn't matter to them. My pop used to tell me never to argue with drunks or fools, so I let it go. They didn't understand logic when they were sober. Now that they were high, it was even worse. I said bye and left.

The next day at school, everybody was questioned. I got called in three times. Nobody was talking. Most of them didn't know anything anyway. Maybe only the Conquistadors knew what really happened; the rest were just hearing rumors. Rumors can take on a life of their own in middle school. A few of them had me surprised at their stupidity. Some said that some high schoolers were trying to pull a Columbine and it went all wrong. Some said a generator blew up, so that's why we were locked down. A kid named Roy jumped on that rumor, putting himself in the story. He said his pop, who worked for the power company, got called in to work on it. The craziest rumor that day was from a girl named Kay. She said that she heard that it was a military operation. As she told it, Homeland Security had found some terrorists on campus and came in to get them. She added that the reason nobody knew who set off the smoke bombs was that it was a classified national security secret. She had the part right about the terrorists, I thought. Only they weren't some foreign-based group that hated America. They were just some local group called the Conquistadors that hated going to school.

For better or worse, it was easy to lie for the guys. There was a line of us outside the door to the principal's office. Inside were the principal, three officers from the county sheriff's department, and the local police. There was even a guy in a dark suit that some kid said was from the FBI. When it got to be my turn, I went in and lied with ease. Did I know what happened? Where was I when it happened? Did I hear anybody talking about what had happened beforehand? Did anybody at the school strike me as the type who would want to harm the school? I had to laugh inside at that one. On any given day half the kids at the school might want to harm it, I thought. But I didn't joke, not once. I lied with a straight face. The only time I didn't lie was when they asked me what I thought about what had happened. I told them straight up. "It was stupid," and I meant it.

That day Henrietta asked about the lockdown as we walked home. She'd been home sick Wednesday, but she'd seen it on the news. I tried to make it sound more exciting that it was. I left out the parts about wanting to use the bathroom, and added more about the smoke. Because she was so interested, I didn't want to disappoint her with a lame story. I told her that it was still smoking when we were let out, and I even threw in something about seeing a couple of soldiers on schoolgrounds, and that we weren't supposed to talk about it. I took that part from Kay's story about the military operation. I didn't mention that it was just some smoke bombs that the guys set off, which they'd probably gotten from her pop anyway.

Friday finally came, and we were all relieved. Once again I got called into the principal's office for questioning. He was really uptight this time around. The newspapers were going crazy over the fact that the school couldn't figure out who set off the smoke bombs. Once again, I lied. I thought that it was just a part of growing up, lying for your friends. Maybe that's how the world ran, I thought. Jesus got hung on the cross for telling the truth, and he was God's son. I didn't want to think of what might happen to me.

The guys were cool that day and didn't get into any trouble. We went to our classes. We went to lunch. And soon it was over. Spring break was on.

Chapter 10

THE FIRST AFTERNOON OF SPRING break, all I could think about was not having to be a Conquistador. I could be away from the guys and be myself. The drugs and stupidity were behind me. Henrietta was coming over to watch movies. We'd watch movies and eat, and everything would be cool. My plans made a fast detour as soon as I walked through my front door.

"Manny!" my abuela called out as I made my way up the stairs.

"Yeah?"

"Cisco is coming over tonight. His parents want me to baby-sit. But we can't say babysit once he gets here. They're going to a wedding rehearsal."

Babysit! I thought. Didn't Cisco's parents know he was already partying and running around on the streets?

"Okay," I mumbled, and went on up to my room.

Cisco stayed out late most school nights, hanging around the cul de sac with the guys. He'd come home sometimes at eleven or twelve smelling like herb. They had to have noticed his tattoos by now. They'd had sons before who ended up in trouble. They should be seeing a pattern—they couldn't possibly believe that he was still a baby. And then to ask my abuela to babysit him! He had his own abuelas that lived around the neighborhood.

I gamed for the rest of the afternoon, then washed up and got ready for Henrietta and Cisco to come over. My abuela made popcorn like she always did when Henrietta and I watched movies. She heated up frozen pizza, too. I tried to lighten up and hope for the best. What if Cisco came over and it was the old Cisco and not the new Conquistador Cisco? We might have a good time. Maybe he'd see that we didn't have to be wannabe gangsters to hang out. I still wondered sometimes if it was really the Conquistadors that had the problem, or if it was me. Maybe they were all growing up in the right way, and I was stuck in the past. Maybe I was the one who was the misfit. When Cisco got to the house, I decided it didn't matter. I didn't want to be like them. He was stoned.

From the minute he got to the house, I knew something was up. His mom and pop didn't even come to the door. They honked the horn and dropped him off. I got the feeling they might have known he was smashed, and they just wanted to get rid of him for the night. He came over before Henrietta got there so I had time to size him up. His eyes were red and glassy. He moved around strangely. I thought he might have been drunk, but then I smelled that smell on him. He was clumsy and loud. Even though it was just me and my abuela in the house, he was talking to us like we were hard of hearing. Every now and then I glanced over at my abuela. She didn't let it faze her. She kept smiling and served him soda and a bowl of popcorn. She had to have noticed, I thought.

Eventually Henrietta arrived. Her mom and baby sister came in like they usually did. My abuela chatted in the kitchen with Henrietta's mom until they left. And Cisco kept goofing.

For a while I thought that he must have been high on herb *and* on speed. It was like he had no self-control. He started to make rude comments about Henrietta and me. Then, as Henrietta and I sat on the couch with Cisco, he became secretive all of sudden and started whispering to us. He wanted to know how long Henrietta's mom and baby sister were going to be there. Then he wanted to know how long my abuela was going to be around. When I told him she stayed in the kitchen the whole time while Henrietta and I watched movies, he sighed and rolled his eyes.

It turns out Cisco wanted to sneak out and meet the guys at the cul de sac. He figured he'd be able to go when my abuela went upstairs or something. He'd promised the guys that he'd meet up with them. If he could just see himself, I thought, he'd wonder why he needed to get higher. It was sad to have him there with us. Henrietta tried to ignore him most of the time. When she couldn't, she'd turn and look at me like I knew what to do, which I didn't. Watching him was like seeing somebody drowning.

Henrietta and I counted the minutes until the movie was over. We'd barely watched any of it. We'd barely eaten any of the pizza or the popcorn my abuela had made. Cisco tapped his foot and waited, too. All he had on his mind, I imagined, was getting to the cul de sac and getting more stoned with the guys. It was sad to think of them all like that. Five minutes before his parents were due to pick him up, he whispered to me on the couch, "Hey, Manny?"

"Yeah."

"Check this out. Big party at the cul de sac tomorrow night. Everybody is going to be there."

By everybody, I guessed he meant the Conquistadors and any other kids who wanted to get high with them.

"So?" I replied.

"You in?"

"I can't. I—I have something to do."

I thought fast for an excuse. Usually on Saturday nights, Henrietta or Bernard would come over to game with me or sometimes both. I hadn't asked either one of them. It was kind of like an understood thing.

"Why not?" Cisco asked. "It's going to be off the hook, man."

"I'm having people over."

"Who?"

"Me," Henrietta interrupted.

I'd never known her to be that crafty. She broke the whole momentum of Cisco trying to convince me to go. I was glad she was there.

"Yeah. Her," I said.

"Ah, man. Your wife? Well, bring her with you, man."

"I can't. We have plans."

"Shhh. Forget you, man!" Cisco replied and shook his head.

Just then a car horn went off in front of the house. Cisco jumped up.

"All right. Peace out," Cisco said.

Even high, he still remembered to thank my abuela for the food and stuff, which surprised me. Then he left.

"OMG," Henrietta sighed as he left out the front door. "He was so messed up."

"Shhh," I said, pointing to my abuela who seemed not to have heard.

My abuela sat at the kitchen table, reading the newspaper. I wondered if her age was starting to show. After Henrietta left, when I was helping her clean up, she started talking. She had that same hurt tone in her voice she'd had when she asked me months ago if I was in a gang.

"Your friend is having problems, Manny. Those are the kinds of problems that you don't need to have," she said, putting away the leftovers.

"I know," I replied.

"Vasco had those problems, too. You know where it got him," she said, making the sign of the cross.

"I know."

"I hope you do," she added. After that, she didn't say anything else.

She had made her point.

I couldn't sleep that night for a long time. I wondered if Cisco had snuck out after he got home and met up with the guys at the cul de sac. It was late already. They might still be out there, I thought. With all of them high, and acting like fools, who would be there to tell them it was time to go home? Maybe they'd pass out up there. That might be a good thing, I decided, cause then they'd have to answer for it. That might shake some sense into them.

Eventually I drifted off to sleep. I actually dreamed that night, which is rare. I dreamed I was in Mexico with my mom and pop, and that I was happy and not worried. There were no Conquistadors there. It was just them and me. My mom was weeding out the garden, and my dad was working on something in the garage.

I woke up to sunlight in my room. It was morning. I dreaded going to school and having to be an again, but then I remembered it was Saturday, the first Saturday of spring break. I jumped out of bed. There were so many things I wanted to do.

After breakfast I went outside to meet Bernard. He was waiting for me across the street, doing tricks on his board in the driveway, just like when I'd first met him. We were going to the north side of town. We'd never ridden that far before. We were going up by the country club. The houses were bigger and more expensive, with really nice cars sitting in the driveways. There were some rolling hills up there that were fun to ride. We skated hard, and covered the ground from our neighborhood to the country club quickly. I felt free, like I was leaving all the stupidity of the Conquistadors back in our neighborhood. It couldn't touch me.

Bernard was right. There were a lot of wild roads up there to ride. They had sweet dips and turns. We could pick up speed and go down low on the boards. There wasn't much traffic so it seemed like our own outdoor skate park, except that they were real roads we were riding on. The golf course looked so peaceful as we passed it. It looked like a park, a lush, secluded, and private park. It would've been fun to explore around in there, I thought. But I decided it wasn't worth the trouble. We could get busted for trespassing, and that would be the end of spring break. I'd be on restriction at home.

We rode around the country club for a couple of hours. Every now and then we'd pass other kids skating or walking and we'd nod. I picked that up from Bernard. Everybody he passed he'd glance at and dip his head and nod. When I first noticed him doing it, I thought he knew everybody he was nodding at, but he didn't. He told me he was just saying hi. It was so different from the Conquistadors' way of doing things. With the Conquistadors, when you passed somebody, you wanted to come off as tough, so you mad-dogged them with a glare.

That morning was a blast. Eventually we headed back home. We rode down Lakeside Avenue, then made a left on Truman. We stopped for drinks and ice cream, and by then it was two in the afternoon. My abuela might worry if we stayed out any later, so I convinced Bernard it was time to go home. He was cool with that, though his mother didn't trip over him being out too long. It wasn't because she didn't care. Bernard was just the kind of kid that you didn't worry about. He avoided trouble. He was cool with everybody, and everybody was cool with him. Well, that's what I thought until we were heading back and made the turn onto Ohio Avenue—and ran smack dab into two Conquistadors.

"Manny!" Hernan yelled out.

I almost ran into him on the sidewalk, making my turn onto Ohio Avenue. I stumbled over my board to stop. Hernan and Cisco were walking down the street, carrying grocery bags.

"Hey, what's up?"

Hernan and Cisco didn't speak for a moment. Instead they sized up Bernard. Bernard stayed on his board and did a 360. Then he nodded to the guys.

"What are you, a skater now?" Hernan asked me with a chuckle.

"We're riding around," I said.

"Who's your friend?—¿Quién es el mayate?" Cisco asked.

I couldn't believe it. I honestly didn't think one of my friends would say that. *Mayate* wasn't a nice word for black people. It was pretty much equal to saying the N-word. I looked over to Bernard, who was doing tricks on his board. He didn't seem to notice. At least I hoped he didn't notice.

"He's my friend. His name is Bernard," I replied.

"What's with that beanie on his head?" Cisco chuckled.

I hung out with Bernard so much, I didn't notice his beanie anymore.

"It's his hat. He likes it," I said.

"Check it out, *ése!*" Hernan held open the grocery bag he was carrying. It had two twelve-packs of beer in it. Cisco held his bag open, too, and it had the same thing inside.

"You're gonna get busted, man," I said immediately.

"By who?" Hernan replied.

I thought about it for a split second and decided he was right. Nobody in their right mind would ever think for a second that two twelve-year old kids would be walking around in broad daylight with four twelve-packs of beer.

"What's it for?" I asked.

"The party tonight, fool," Cisco interjected. "I told you it was going to be off the hook."

"So, you coming?" questioned Hernan.

"No. I can't. I'm having people over."

"Who, the *mayate*?" Hernan said.

Now they were going too far. I felt my face start to flush with anger. I'd never hit anybody out of anger, especially one of my best friends, but at that moment I wanted to. I looked at Bernard. He was sitting on the curb staring in the other direction, waiting for me. I made a quick, silent prayer to God that Bernard hadn't heard him.

"People. I'm having people over."

"Man, it's gonna be cool. Some eighth-grade girls are coming, man. Bring your friend if you want," Hernan coaxed.

"I can't," I said, and left it at that.

"All right. More for us!" cheered Cisco.

"I'll see you guys," I said, then turned around.

"Later, man." The guys walked on.

I tapped Bernard on the shoulder. He hopped up, threw his board onto the street, jumped on, and sailed off. I did the same.

When we got back to our street it was after three. I was tired and wanted to take a nap. We'd covered twenty miles at least that day. I asked Bernard if he wanted to come over later and game. He said he couldn't because he and his mom were going out to eat. I said I'd see him in the morning for Mass, then turned around and headed toward my house. I stopped as I remembered I had to apologize for what the guys had said.

"Bernard!"

Bernard was already at his front door across the street when I caught him. He turned and hollered back, "Yeah?"

"Sorry about what the guys said. They're stupid sometimes!"

"That's okay. Some of my friends are jerks, too!"

I laughed when he said that. He waved and went inside.

From that point on, spring break rocked. I hung out with Bernard or Henrietta every day. I gamed, sometimes all night. On Wednesday, the three of us went to the big amusement park. We got there at eleven and stayed past eleven at night. We went on almost every ride. We ate everything we saw. The whole time we were there I kept thinking about how miserable it would have been if the Conquistadors had been there, too. We'd probably have gotten kicked out of the park. Everything the Conquistadors did seemed like a challenge: Was I cool enough to do it? It wasn't like that with Bernard or Henrietta. They just wanted to have fun.

Because my abuela said she was too old to run around the park all day, she sat in a coffee shop reading the paper most of the time. She met an older abuelo there who was doing the same thing. They chatted in Spanish almost from morning till night. I was glad she had someone to talk to. When I stopped by every now and then to check in with her, she almost made it seem like I was getting in the way of her conversation. Time flew by, and before I knew it we were in the car, driving home. We were so tired that we slept for most of the ride.

The next day I woke up with a fun hangover. I was groggy and sore. After breakfast I took my soccer ball and skated down to the park. Since Bernard went to Catholic school, his spring break schedule didn't match mine. He'd spent Wednesday with us only as a special occasion. And with Henrietta spending the day shopping with her mom, I was by myself. I didn't bother to call up any of the Conquistadors to see what they were doing. I knew what they would want to do if I called. When I got to the park, I shot goals for about a half hour, and did some dribbling drills for another half hour. I was heading home when the unthinkable happened. The Conquistadors showed up.

They were their usual goofy and high selves as they told me all about the party on Saturday night. Bartolomeu could hardly control himself when he got to the part about how high they'd gotten. He stumbled and spun around when he was pretending to be Cisco. Then Nando got all ecstatic, telling me how he and some eighth-grade goth-girl ended up kissing before the party was over. I tried to pretend to be interested, but that was getting to be a hard job with the Conquistadors. I didn't bother to tell them about going to the park the day before. They probably wouldn't have been interested. Just as I was getting ready to say bye—they were heading off to the cul de sac—they started again.

"Manny! We're having another party this Saturday night. You have to be there!" Hernan ordered.

"What?" I replied.

"We don't care what your excuse is. You're coming!" added Cisco.

"No way. I got stuff to do," I argued.

"This is Conquistadors' business. You have to be there—" Bartolomeu was saying when Hernan cut him off.

"Shut up, man. Shut up!"

Hernan threw an arm around my shoulder and walked me a few steps away from the other guys. Then, of all things, he got real with me. It kind of shocked me. I hadn't seen the real Hernan in months. Away from the guys, he spoke to me in a genuine and honest way.

"Hey, Manny. We're just saying it's going to be fun and we want our homeboy there. Forget those other guys and stuff. You, me, and Cisco go back, right? We just want our friend there, is all. We know you don't party with us, and that's cool. But just pass by and say hey or something, all right? Bring your hippie friend. Bring your girlfriend, too. It's all good. Okay?"

What could I say? He was my old friend Hernan. He'd always be my old friend Hernan, no matter what. It didn't seem like I'd be saying no to the Conquistadors just then if I didn't go. It seemed like I'd be saying no to friendship, and our past friendship even. It would be like disrespecting something honorable.

"All right. We'll pass by," I said to Hernan, out of earshot of the guys.

"What's he saying?" Nando called out to Hernan.

"He's in!" Hernan shouted back.

The rest of the guys cheered. And that was the only time I felt good about it, that moment when I'd said yes. Seconds later, as I was on my board and riding home, the dread started to sink in. I'd said it and now I had to go through with it. It was Thursday, and I knew that time flew by when something bad was coming. It would seem like only minutes before it was Saturday night. The last few days of my vacation were gone.

Chapter 11

JUST AS I'D FEARED, SATURDAY came faster than any day had ever come in my life. I'd been miserable since Thursday morning. I asked Bernard to come with me, but he balked at going. He said it wasn't his scene and that he'd see me in the morning for church. Luckily Henrietta agreed to go. She'd said it would be easier for me to leave quickly with her there.

The plan was that we were going to go by at about nine, hang out for fifteen or twenty minutes, and then leave. There'd be some eighth-grade goth girls there that Henrietta didn't get along with. They dressed all in black, smoked cigarettes, and wore jewelry with skulls and spiders and things on them. The goth girls had more tattoos than any wannabe gangster. Their makeup was all black, nail polish too, and even their eye shadow and lipstick. And even though their hair might be black to begin with, they would dye it to make it look even blacker. Sometimes they'd add blue or orange streaks. The goth girls would listen to their mp3 players all day long, even in class. They were always getting busted for listening to music in class or for smoking, but they didn't care.

It seemed like almost every day after school there'd be a group of them waiting outside the principal's office for their parents to pick them up. And people said they liked to party. That's why Hernan and Cisco and the rest of the Conquistadors had made friends with them, I guessed.

That Saturday night I waited on the porch for Henrietta. She was walking over by herself, so we didn't have to worry about lying to her mom about where we were going. I'd told my abuela that we were going to the park for a little while. I carried my soccer ball with me so it wouldn't seem like a lie. My abuela didn't seem suspicious. She just told me not to be out late.

Henrietta finally arrived a little before nine. I tossed the soccer ball into the bushes in front of my abuela's house, and we set out right away for the cul de sac, which was about a mile from our neighborhood. We didn't say much. We each knew what the other was thinking. She knew I didn't want to go, and I knew she didn't want to hang out with those goth girls. Henrietta was a girly-girl who wore pink and put little hearts all over her homework and stuff. She even still liked dolls. She thought the goth girls were dumb, and they felt the same about her clique of friends.

As we approached the cul de sac, we both got nervous. Henrietta grabbed my hand. I was glad, because I'd wanted to grab onto her hand, but I didn't want to look scared. We could hear voices in the near distance. I also began to smell that smell. There were a few lights at the end of the cul de sac. They looked like some solar garden lights—the guys had probably stolen them from someone's yard for the party. We got closer and saw about twenty people there. They had a ghetto blaster playing rock songs. Some kids were sitting on the curb right in the middle of the cul de sac, and a few were standing around. The guys all had cans of beer in their hands. The closer we got, the stupider it looked. The goth girls were there. Henrietta groaned under her breath.

"Manny!" Nando cried out as he saw me approaching. He held a can of beer high in the air. He looked wasted.

Kids looked us over as we walked into the party. Then they went back to whatever it was they were doing. There were about ten goth girls, the Conquistadors, and few other random faces. Ferdinand came up and gave me a bro-shake, then slung his arm over my shoulder. I think he did it because he couldn't stand up straight on his own. He smelled like beer and that smell, and he had a big goofy smile on his face.

"Heyyy, *vato*," he said.

He took a spare beer out of his pocket and handed it to me. I took the can, but I didn't want to drink it. I just held it.

"What's up, man?" I asked him out of habit.

"It's a good party, man."

Suddenly we heard what sounded like choking. I looked through the darkness to a half-finished model house and made out Bartolomeu. He was hunched over and puking. The whole party turned to look. One person after another started busting out with laughter. They all thought it was funny to see him that sick. Once again, I was sad. Looking over to Henrietta, I saw that her eyes were darting from place to place. She couldn't fix her gaze on anything, because she didn't want to look. I knew that feeling.

"Manny!" Hernan yelled out.

He was sitting with some goth girls on the curb, smack dab in the middle of the cul de sac. He and the girls were giggling and laughing and acting stupid. I could hear Hernan trying to explain to the girls who I was.

"That's my homeboy, Manny! We've been friends since kindergarten. He's a solid Conquistador!"

Hernan was drunk. He was slurring and talking nonsense. He stayed seated when I got near him, probably because he couldn't stand up. Cisco was sitting cross-legged right behind him on the sidewalk. He and a goth girl were all hunched over, whispering something. Cisco had a strange, paranoid look about him. Hernan seemed like the old Hernan in a way, except that he was wasted. But Cisco seemed like an alien. I wondered, was it the booze, or herb, or speed that was making him act like that? The goth girls must've brought their own booze because they all had a bottle of fizzy strawberry wine in their hands. Glancing back to Henrietta, I could see that she wanted to leave right away.

"Let me just say hi real fast and then we'll go," I reassured her.

She nodded and grabbed my hand even tighter. We walked over to where Hernan and Cisco were sitting. I stooped down to give Hernan a bro-shake, then tried to give one to Cisco, too, but all he did was nod at my hand and go back to whispering with the goth girl.

"We gotta roll, man. Just wanted to say hi," I said.

"It's cool, man. It's cool," Hernan slurred out.

I wondered if they'd even remember we were there. Feeling free to leave, I turned around and pulled Henrietta with me.

As we started to walk away, I began to see two T-shirted bodies bouncing around in the distance. They were coming up the road that led to the cul de sac. White T-shirts and baggy jeans were all I could make out in the darkness. At first I thought it was a couple of Conquistadors, but then I realized that all the Conquistadors were already here at the base of the cul de sac. One approaching body looked bigger than the other. As a light shone across their faces, I made out that it was Carl and Victor.

This was bad, I thought, like playing with matches around a gas station.

Victor and Carl were really moving. I could tell they meant business by the way they were walking up the street. They had their orange caps on.

I felt lightheaded. And still, Henrietta's hand pulled me along as we continued to walk away. As Carl and Victor got closer, they recognized me.

"Manny, are your friends here?" Carl asked sternly.

I choked out, "I—I," but nothing more would come out. I couldn't speak. As we passed each other, Henrietta tugged me even harder.

"Keep walking, Manny," she said.

I didn't want to stop and turn around, but that's exactly what I did.

For a brief second I thought it was going to be all right. Hernan was so high he was giddy. When he saw Carl and Victor, he seemed genuinely happy to see them. He staggered to his feet and shook hands with them. I could hear him being nice to them from where I was standing.

"My *vatos*! Get some beers, guys! Come on. It's a party!" he slurred out.

Carl and Victor looked puzzled. Even they thought the condition that the guys were in was pitiful.

"We just came for my money, man," Carl said.

Bending down, Hernan grabbed up a bottle of the fizzy strawberry wine from one of the goth girls.

"Come on. Have a drink," Hernan said. He shoved the bottle of wine toward them. "It's a party. It's the last party of spring break!"

Then something went wrong. In trying to hand the bottle to one of the guys, Hernan dropped it accidentally. *Krashlink!* The bottle fell to the ground and scattered broken glass all over the place. There was a brief second when everybody just stopped what they were doing and waited. I could see Hernan's drunken eyes. They were blank and confused. I'm not sure he even understood what had happened. The blank look suddenly turned to rage as Hernan leapt at Carl like a cheetah taking down a gazelle. His fists swung so fast I couldn't count the times he hit Carl. Jarred for a split second, Victor just stared until Cisco's two-handed grip grabbed his shirt and flung him to the ground. The goth girls began to scream. There was cursing and panic everywhere. And still, Harnon and Cisco continued to pummel Carl and Victor. They had each one down on the ground and they kept hitting them. I heard Henrietta scream out my name. Then she yanked me so hard she could have pulled my arm out of its socket. She just kept pulling and dragging me away.

I could see that Bartolomeu was still down on his hands and knees from puking, and Nando and Ferdinand were in a state of drunken, wide-eyed shock. The screaming from the girls continued. Next thing I knew, Henrietta and I were running. It started out as a light jog, but soon we were sprinting away from the cul de sac. Neither of us said anything. There was nothing we could do. It took us about ten minutes of straight running until we were back to our neighborhood.

When we reached the corner of my block, we stopped. Hunched over on our hands and knees, huffing and puffing, we waited. What we were waiting for, neither of us knew.

"What do we do?" Henrietta asked.

"I don't know."

"We have to do something."

"I know. I—I can't tell my abuela."

"I'll tell my mom. I'll tell her we were at the park and some kids rode by on bikes and said there was a big fight at the cul de sac."

"What's she gonna do?"

"She'll call the police."

"We'd be ratting!"

"We have to."

"All right. Don't say we saw anything!"

"I won't."

Henrietta kissed me on the cheek, then went off. Seeing her walk away made me feel scared. She'd been there with me and had seen it all, too. I didn't want to be left with all that on my own. I didn't want to go home and have my abuela see my face. She'd see in my eyes that something bad had happened. Catching my breath, I waited until Henrietta disappeared down the street.

Gathering up my courage, I stood up straight and walked home. I tried to act normal. But as soon as I walked through the door, my knew something was up.

"Manny, what happened?"

"Nothing," I said, out of habit.

"You look scared, like you saw a ghost or something."

"I, we—we were at the park, and some kids rode by on bikes real scared and said there was a fight at some cul de sac."

"What?"

"That's what they said so we ran all the way home."

"Oh my heavens!" my abuela shrieked.

She covered her mouth with her hands and had a wide-eyed look shock on her face.

"Do you know who it was?"

"No."

"I have to call the police or something."

"Henrietta's mom is already doing that."

"Oh my heavens," my abuela repeated.

She suddenly grabbed me and hugged me real tight. I could feel from the hug that the news had scared her. Suddenly we heard the sounds of distant sirens heading in the direction of the cul de sac.

"Oh my heavens," my abuela kept saying. "You don't know who they are?"

"No."

"You didn't see anything?"

"No."

My abuela made me go into the kitchen to eat some soup. We didn't say much. I think she just wanted to keep her eyes on me, like if she didn't see me, I might end up getting hurt somehow. I didn't mind, 'cause I didn't want to be alone. Sure, it hurt not to tell my abuela the truth, but there'd be no way to explain it to her.

Two big bowls of soup later, my abuela decided to call Henrietta's mom. She lightened up on the phone, so I was able to relax a little. She spoke quickly in Spanish and I overheard her saying how scared I was, and I could tell Henrietta's mom was saying the same thing about her daughter. My abuela even laughed a little. I could tell it was a laugh of relief.

My abuela sent me up to bed right afterward.

"No gaming. No TV," she ordered.

I knew she wasn't punishing me, that she just wanted me to get some rest because I'd been through a lot. If she had known the truth, though, it would have been a punishment order for sure. I didn't argue with her—part of me felt like if I fell asleep and woke up all over again, that it would be like it was all just a bad dream.

Sunday morning was gray. As my eyes opened, the dimness of the light made me wonder what time of day it was. Had I slept all day and now it was evening again? I tried not to remember what had happened, but the details started coming back to me. I could see Hernan's fists pummeling Carl, and Cisco thrashing Victor. Pulling me back to reality, my abuela called out her usual Sunday orders from downstairs.

"Manny, get ready for church. I don't want to be late!" she yelled up to my room.

"Okay," I mumbled, dragging myself out of bed.

The ride to church was quiet. Bernard rode with us, and I think he sensed something was up. Feeling that I wasn't in the mood to goof, he didn't either. After church we had hamburgers at the restaurant we usually went to when Bernard was with us. Once again I couldn't taste my food. One of the worst parts about having a guilty conscience, I thought, was not being able to taste the food you like. I barely ate two bites of my burger. My abuela had the waitress put it in a box for me to eat later, and after Bernard was finished with his lunch, we left for home.

My abuela got a phone call as soon as we were in. It was one of her gossip buddies, another abuela from a couple of neighborhoods away. As I sat on the couch in the family room, watching TV, I could hear my abuela's one-sided conversation. It was about the fight that had happened last night. My abuela's sighs and "Oh my heavens" were telling me that the details of the night were beginning to unfold. Would *my* name come up? I wondered. Maybe one of the other kids would say I had been there. I suffered through the conversation for about twenty minutes until my abuela said *adios* and hung up the phone.

"Oh my heavens," she sighed, putting the phone down. "Manny, I have some bad news."

"What is it?" I asked, feeling relieved that she wasn't yelling at me, that she hadn't found out I had been there.

My abuela put her hands over her mouth, and shook her head. She had a look of disbelief on her face.

"Manny, your friend Carl, the big one?"

"Yeah?"

"He's in the hospital. He's all beat up. He was one of the people that was hurt in that fight last night."

"What?" fell out of my mouth.

"Him and another boy named Victor. They're both in the hospital. They're hurt bad. They can't even speak. Broken jaws. Broken noses. It's serious."

I wanted to cry. Victor and Carl had been good friends. I felt like I had hurt them, and that I was continuing to hurt them.

"Shhh. Who did it?"

"The police don't know yet. When they got to the scene, all they found were the boys on the ground. They called the paramedics, who took them right to the hospital. They said there'd been some party or something. There were bottles and cans all over the place. They think maybe the Playaz were having a party and your friends got caught up in some trouble."

Beginning to feel worse, I got up to hide in the bathroom.

"I gotta go," I said to my abuela, then left the room.

In the bathroom, I locked the door and sat down on the floor. Letting my head droop down, I closed my eyes. What a mess everything was. The Playaz were going to get dragged into something that they had nothing to do with. Who knows what could happen when a real gang like the Playaz got mad because they were accused of something they didn't do? And Carl and Victor. What about them? Their parents don't even know the truth. The whole thing was going to get messier. The cops would figure out that Carl and Victor were in the Playaz by what they were wearing. They'd realize that the Playaz wouldn't knock out two of their own.

"Manny! Telephone! It's Henrietta."

I got off the floor and left the bathroom. I grabbed the phone from my abuela and went upstairs to my room. Squatting down on the floor, I leaned my head back against the bed.

"Hear the news?" Henrietta asked.

"Yeah. Did you say anything?" I whispered into the phone.

"No. My mom tipped off the cops on a stolen cell phone she got from my dad. He's so crazy, he's always got stuff like that. Then she threw it into the wash today to get rid of it. She doesn't want to be known as a rat."

"Carl and Victor are in the hospital," I said.

"I know. The news is all over town. I'm just surprised nobody ratted on your friends yet."

"You think anybody will?"

"I don't know. I'm not saying anything to anybody. Those goth girls can be loud sometimes. Who knows what's going to happen with them? Or maybe Carl and Victor will say something? Who knows?"

"Yeah. Who knows?" I repeated.

"Everything is going to be okay. Don't worry. You didn't do anything. I'll tell anybody that."

"That doesn't matter. We know what happened. That's enough."

"So are you going to rat?" she asked.

"No!" I said, and I meant it. No matter what, I wouldn't rat.

"See you tomorrow."

"Bye."

After hanging up the phone, I stayed up in my room in the

same position for what seemed like hours. Tomorrow was going to be Monday, I remembered. Spring break was over. It felt like guilt was eating its way from my middle out. I thought about Victor's and Carl's parents standing around their sons' hospital beds. I imagined they had to be feeling ten times worse than I was feeling. The guys didn't get caught, and now who knows what they were doing? Since the cul de sac was too hot to party at, they were probably down in the wash right now getting high. They were getting high, and everybody else was suffering. What kind of messed-up deal was that?

Chapter 12

MONDAY WAS ANOTHER GRAY, CLOUDY day. So much for spring, I thought as I walked to school that morning. It was as if the sky was frowning in disgust. Of course, I didn't want to go to school. I knew it was going to be bad, especially if nobody had ratted yet. The principal, vice principal, teachers, and cops—everybody would be scurrying around like crazy trying to figure out just what happened.

And that's exactly what I walked into as I entered the gates of school. I didn't have to worry about dealing with the guys and having to listen to their stupidity, because there were yard duty teachers everywhere. The principal himself was out in the quad with a bullhorn, walking around. There were a couple of cops standing by the door of the office. Most of the kids were told to go line up for their regular classes. We couldn't socialize. We had to go straight to our first period classes. I glanced at the guys goofing around near the basketball courts. They were all there. Hernan was wearing shades like nothing was up. Out of reflex, I looked over to where Carl and Victor usually stood in the mornings. The area was coldly empty. The goth girls were running around in their little pack, hunched over and whispering excitedly. They wouldn't be able to keep a secret long, I thought. It was just a matter of time. I nodded to the guys and went to my first period class, as if it were a normal day.

Inside the classroom, I sat down at my desk. As I was putting my backpack under my seat, I noticed Henrietta sitting at her desk across the room. She glanced at me with a look like, well, here goes. I felt the same way. As soon as the first bell rang, the announcements came over the loudspeakers. All the usual troublemakers were called up to the office. I heard all of the Conquistadors' names except for mine, Ferdinand's, and Nando's. I hadn't thought to look when I first sat down, but now I turned around to see if Ferdinand was in his seat. He was there, trying to look busy by scribbling in his notebook. Nobody was going to rat, I thought. It would have to come right from Carl's or Victor's lips, or the truth would never come out. The goth girls might let it slip, too, I reminded myself. I settled into class and tried to concentrate.

Second period was just like first. The bell rang and more announcements were made. More troublemakers were called up to the office. I was spared from the cut once again. But it also meant that the truth hadn't come out yet, otherwise the announcements would've stopped, I figured. Hernan, Cisco, and Bartolomeu must've already been questioned, and lied through their teeth. Hernan probably did it with a goofy smile on his face. Cisco would've done his lying defiantly, with an attitude. And Bartolomeu, he probably just played dumb, which was not a real stretch for him.

By third period, I knew I was due. Right after the bell, my heart starting beating faster as I waited to hear the distorted speaker of the overhead intercom. Just like I'd anticipated, the speaker popped on and the secretary rattled off a list of names. All I heard was *da-da-da*, ". . . and Manny, please report to the principal's office." There it was, I thought. I'm done for. I closed my books, put my pencil in my backpack, stood up and pulled it up over my shoulder, and left the classroom.

As I walked to the principal's office, I began to feel dizzy and nauseous—which was becoming a regular feeling for me, almost every day since the Conquistadors had started. Inside the office, I gulped down hard and sat down in a chair between two other kids. No goth girls were in the waiting room. If I did decide to tell the truth, I couldn't do it until I knew some goth girls had been there. What are you thinking? I scolded myself. You can't rat!

One by one, kids were called into the principal's office. While kids were coming in and out and the door hung open, I noticed that the office was full of uniformed bodies. Some were tan and green, which meant county sheriffs. And some were all black with blue trim, which meant local police. Even the smoke bomb prank wasn't this bad. If the truth got out, somebody would most likely end up in juvie. Hernan and Cisco better pray this doesn't get out, I was thinking when the secretary called out my name.

As soon as I stood on my feet, I wanted to puke. It was right at the back of my throat. I couldn't let that happen with all those kids in the waiting room. I forced it down my throat and walked into the principal's office.

The principal gave the cops a brief rundown of my background. I was surprised at what he was saying about me.

"This is Manny. Seventh grade. Twelve years old. 'A' student. High Achiever. No suspensions. No referrals. Intramural soccer team. Likes to game. Friends with the two victims. Also on file as being associated with or involved with the Conquistadors gang, although he's recorded on file as denying any such relationship."

Wow, I thought. I'd never heard anybody sum up my life like that. Just a few lines and yet it was everything about me. It made me feel small, like my life wasn't even worth a full paragraph. I couldn't think too long about it, because the questions began. Did I know the victims? Were we friends? Had I ever been to a cul de sac on so and so street? Was I hanging out with them Saturday night? Did I know anybody who had hung out with them Saturday night? Had I heard about what happened Saturday night? Did I know the victims were in the hospital? Did I know if the victims were involved in any gang activity? Could I think of anybody who had a beef with the victims? Could I think of anybody who bought or sold alcohol for young people? Did I know of any drug-related activity occurring on school grounds? They left no stone unturned.

As I walked out of the principal's office, I was so exhausted I wanted a nap. My hands and underarms were drenched. I shuffled off to class and wished the day was over. When it finally did end, I felt relieved. I walked home with Henrietta. Neither one of us said a thing. She hadn't been called in to the principal's office, and I had. I had the story to tell, but I didn't want to talk about it. She seemed to understand and left it alone.

Later that night she called me on the phone. By that time, I was ready to talk. I told her all about the cops and the questioning. She told me all about those loony goth girls and what they were saying in the PE locker room. She'd overheard them talking about the fight.

"Right after we left, Hernan and Cisco stopped beating up Carl and Victor. Their faces were all bloody and they were out cold. Everybody got scared and ran off," Henrietta said.

I asked Henrietta why the goth-girls hadn't been called into the principal's office, and she acted like I was stupid or something.

"Don't you know?"

"What?"

"Nobody believes anything those girls say. They get in trouble and lie so much, nobody takes anything they say seriously."

My hopes were dashed with those words. I hated to admit it, but I was secretly hoping the goth girls would talk. I wanted everybody to know what had happened, even if it was my friends who were on the line. It wasn't right. Feeling depressed, I hung up the phone.

After getting ready for bed, I climbed in and stared at the ceiling. Maybe Carl and Victor would be feeling better tomorrow. I hoped they would. Then they could tell what had happened. Why couldn't I just go along with it, I wondered. Why did my conscience make me sick, and Hernan's and Cisco's didn't?

The next day on my way to school, I felt weak. I hadn't eaten a full meal since Saturday morning. My abuela was worried and wanted to take me to the doctor, but I told her I'd make sure to eat my whole lunch. The scene at the gates of the school was exactly like it was the day before. No socializing and no games. Kids were in single file lines right in front of their classroom doors. I didn't see the guys. They must've already lined up for class, I guessed. I made my way to my first period classroom and waited for the door to open. I felt dizzy but I forced myself to keep it together. I didn't want to embarrass myself by collapsing in line.

Once inside the classroom, I was glad I could sit down. And again, the morning announcements ended with a list of names that were to report to the principal's office. I turned around, and there was Ferdinand scribbling in his notebook like he'd done the day before. He looked cool. Other than trying to look busy, he didn't look bothered at all. Nando was in class, too. He was nodding off, trying to force himself to stay awake, but he was there. I looked across the room, and Henrietta was in her seat whispering to a girlfriend behind her. It was the same day all over again, I thought. Nobody was going to rat. And it would be just like this again tomorrow. Meanwhile, Carl and Victor were in the hospital. After the teacher took attendance, I was about to ask to use the restroom when the intercom popped on again. Another list of names was called out, including mine. I was shocked. I hadn't expected to get called in again so soon. Maybe somebody said something about me, like they'd known I'd been there at the cul de sac that night. As I gathered up my things into my backpack, I began to feel dizzy again.

I walked out of the room and started across the quad to the office. I was so weak; the office looked a million miles away. I struggled to keep my vision focused. Then, halfway between the classroom and the office, right in the middle of the quad, it felt as if all the life in me just evaporated into thin air. I couldn't see. I felt myself falling. It felt as if I was falling for a long time, just sinking into the ground. *Thud!* I heard the sound of my body as it hit the ground. Slowly I began to feel the pain from the impact. I'd landed on my shoulder and it throbbed like I'd just run into a block wall. Feeling sleepy, I let myself drift off.

I saw myself back in kindergarten. The details were so real I could even remember that kindergarten smell in the classroom. Everybody was there, the way we were. Hernan was there, and Cisco, too. We were little all over again. At our group table we were cutting out little letters to glue onto our work. We had those little kid kindergarten scissors, but we only had one pair.

We had to pass off the scissors to each other so we could finish our work. Hernan was using them first.

"My turn," Cisco said.

"No, Manny's next," Hernan directed.

Even then he was bossy, I thought. I didn't want the dream to end, so I focused real hard on keeping it going. I wanted to see it for as long as I could. Next thing I knew, we were sitting on a colorful grid rug at the front of the class. All the kids I could remember from kindergarten were there, too, and some I hadn't remembered since. Hernan was sitting on my left and Cisco on my right. We listened hard to the teacher. He had just read us a story about good neighbors, and now he was quizzing us on what it meant. We all wanted to be good neighbors, too. We meant it, too, even Hernan and Cisco. Sensing the dream was ending, I started to feel depressed again. I could feel reality coming closer and the dream slipping away. It was dark. Then my eyes opened.

Scared awake, I wasn't sure what had happened to me. I was lying down in a room and there were people around me. The faces were familiar, but I couldn't place them. Then I saw the school secretary lean inside the room with a puzzled expression.

"Is he all right?" she asked.

"He just fainted. Doesn't look like he hit his head or anything. He fell on his shoulder and backpack."

I noticed the first aid kits and bandages and stuff. I figured I was in the nurse's office. I'd never been in there before, I realized. I sat up quickly.

"Do you feel all right?" the nurse asked.

"Yeah."

"One of the officers who are here today carried you in. We were about to call the paramedics. Your grandma is on her way."

"Okay."

The nurse left me alone in the room and went out in the hall. I could hear her talking with the secretary. They cancelled the ambulance and decided that if I was sick or something, my abuela could take me to the hospital. I was glad. The last thing I wanted to do was go to the hospital. I'd end up in the same room as Carl and Victor. That would torture my conscience to no end.

"Can I get a drink of water?" I called out into the hall.

"Sure. Go ahead," the nurse replied.

I got up and made my way down the hall. There were a lot of kids sitting outside the principal's office. I suddenly remembered why I'd been walking across the quad in the first place. Feeling a familiar sense of misery begin to fall back on me, I sighed, then took a drink of water.

"Manny!" my abuela cried out.

I looked down the hall and saw my abuela running towards me. She looked scared. When she reached me, she grabbed me into a tight hug. I was so embarrassed. There were kids everywhere, and they were seeing the whole thing.

"Are you okay?"

"Yeah, I'm fine. I just need to eat."

"We'll go to the hospital right now."

"No—no—no. I just need to eat something."

Just as we were getting ready to leave, the unbelievable happened. As I looked across the office, I saw two red and somber older faces. My eyes stopped right on them. It was Victor's parents—the drunks. They were waiting in the office for any leads, I guessed. They looked so pitiful. They may have been drunks, but you could tell that they were hurt inside. They cared, I knew. They cared and wanted to know what happened, and I knew and wasn't saying anything. That was it. Seeing Victor's parents' faces was all I could take. I had to tell. I couldn't hold it in. Hernan and Cisco were my friends, but that wasn't enough. Still, I couldn't do it right then, in the office, with all the kids watching me do it.

"Let's go," I said to my abuela.

Chapter 13

A COUPLE OF HOURS AFTER getting home that Tuesday morning, I decided it was time to go to the police station. My abuela had fed me two big bowls of soup with bread. I was full and felt better than I had in a couple of days. My energy was coming back. Even so, my abuela would worry if I left the house right after fainting at school. So I decided not to say anything to her. I'd wait until she was on the phone or something, and then I'd sneak out. I had to go all the way to the middle of the city, and it would take me at least ten minutes by skateboard to get there. Better than walking, I figured. If I walked, it would take me forty minutes at least.

Upstairs, in front of my gamebox, I waited. I listened for sounds downstairs that meant my abuela was occupied with something. Then I got lucky.

She called up the stairs. "Manny! I'm going to the market. I'll be back in an hour. You want anything special?"

"No. I'm all right," I hollered back down.

It was perfect timing, I thought. Couldn't ask for a better window of opportunity. Now I just had to put on my jacket and go. One last time I weighed the pros and cons of what I was about to do. I remembered the dream I'd had when I'd fainted at school. I saw us, the guys, as we used to be. Then I thought about Victor's parents. They were drunks and probably miserable, and maybe the only thing in the world that made them feel better was their son Victor. Slowly I started to feel rotten for not having told the truth sooner. I grabbed my board and left.

I was almost down to the corner of our block when I heard a familiar sound behind me, another skateboard. I stopped and turned to see who it was.

"Hey! What's up, man?" Bernard said as he screeched to a stop behind me.

He was on his spring break and skating around all day. I'd forgotten his schedule. He seemed light and carefree, like he had no idea that the world as I knew it was about to end, that I was about to rat. We were living in parallel universes.

"Hey man," he greeted me. "No school?"

"Nah. I had school. I got sick and came home early. Feeling better now."

"Where you going?"

"I gotta go do something."

"Where ya headed?"

"First Avenue."

"I'll roll with you."

And with that, Bernard took off down the street, me trailing behind as usual. As we skated, I almost started to forget what a mess my life was. It felt like it was Saturday and we were just goofing around like we did most weekends. Only it wasn't the weekend, I recalled, and I wasn't just hanging out. I was heading to First Avenue to go to the police station and tell them what had happened at the cul de sac Saturday night. I didn't mind letting Bernard go with me. He wouldn't rat me out, I decided. Funny, how I was so worried about ratting on people and yet I didn't want anybody to rat on me.

We made it to First Avenue in a few minutes. When we got to the front of the library in the middle of town, Bernard stopped.

"Where ya headed?"

I nodded at the police station across the street. That jarred Bernard for a second.

"What for?" he asked.

"I gotta take care of something."

"Want me to come with you?"

"No. It's cool. Thanks, man. I'll see you later."

I must've looked scared or something 'cause Bernard sensed it. As I stood just looking at the police station, he stayed put. He didn't go anywhere.

"Nah, it's cool. I'll hang out with you. Got no where else to go."

After waiting for a break in the traffic, we crossed the street. The walkway up to the police station looked fifty miles long from the sidewalk. I almost decided not to do it. Forget it, I thought. The truth will come out either way eventually. As I was about to turn around and leave, my stomach tightened up as if my body was telling me to go through with it. It was my conscience attacking me again. It wouldn't let up. I gulped some air and started walking to the station. My legs felt wobbly as I stumbled up to the two big glass doors. I glanced inside and saw that it was empty except for an officer behind the counter.

The officer behind the counter was a woman. She didn't look up as we came through the doors. It was quiet inside the front office, like a library or something. There were little video cameras in every corner. They were watching us, I thought.

Bernard and I walked up to the counter. After a moment the officer behind the desk looked up.

"Yes?" she asked.

"I—I." I coughed to clear my throat. I wasn't sure if I was going to be able to make the words come out of my mouth.

"I want to, um . . . I know what happened at the cul de sac Saturday night."

"What cul de sac?"

"The one where the kids got hurt."

"Wait one moment, please," the officer said. She picked up the phone and pressed a button. Eventually she began to speak.

"There's a young man out here who'd like to make a statement about what occurred on a cul de sac Saturday night."

It was out there now, I thought. There was no way I could take it back. Now it was just a matter of finishing the job. I looked over at Bernard and he nodded—a nod that said he had my back. That felt good. It was the only encouragement I'd felt in wanting to tell the truth. A minute later a plainclothes detective came out to the front office and guided us into the back. He had a dress shirt and a tie on, but he wore a gun and a badge on his belt. I'd never seen a gun that close, and just the look of it scared me. It had the power to kill people. I wondered if he'd ever killed anybody. As we walked through the police station, I remembered taking a tour of it back in second grade. I saw the rifles in the gun locker, the computers, and people walking around doing things. I'd thought it was cool back then. It was different now. Everything meant life and death.

We entered an office with a table and chairs. I sat at a chair at the table, and Bernard sat on one against the wall. There was a second officer waiting for us with a pen and report pad. It was all official now, I knew. It wasn't going to be just middle school gossip in a few minutes. It was going to be for real.

The officers took down our names, addresses, and guardian information. Then they wanted to know what schools Bernard and I went to. Finally they asked for the story. I told them exactly what had happened, as best as I could remember. I thought it was important that they know that Bartolomeu, Nando, and Ferdinand were all too stoned to do anything, and from what I saw they hadn't beat up anybody. The cops seemed surprised that there was so much booze at the party. They asked if I knew where Hernan and Cisco had gotten it from. I told them that I didn't know, and from what I remembered about that day, I didn't want to know. They also wanted to know a lot about where Carl was getting the herb from, or where I thought he might be getting the herb from. I told them the truth, which was that I didn't know. Sometimes it's good not to know things, I thought. I would've ended up ratting on more people. As the information came out, I started to feel more like myself. Over and over, I repeated that this was an anonymous tip, and they kept nodding in agreement. After an hour or so in that office, I noticed my abuela poking her head around inside the police station. The cops must've called her and filled her in on what was going on. Some officers were showing her to the office we were in. She looked scared. When she got inside, she gave me a big hug again.

"Next time you tell me where you're going!" she ordered, her finger pointing at my nose.

"All right."

I finished up the story, and officers seemed pleased. My abuela grabbed my hand and we left with Bernard. It was over, I thought. I'd done it, for better or worse. Oddly, I felt hungry.

On the car ride home, my abuela stayed silent. Every few minutes, she'd shake her head and whisper, "Oh my heavens," then sigh. I knew why she was upset. While telling the whole story to the cops, I'd had to tell them that I had been the drug go-between for the guys. I knew I had broken my abuela's heart.

I found out just how brokenhearted she was when we got home. After we'd said good night to Bernard, and just as soon as she walked through our door, she headed straight for the phone. From the kitchen, I overheard her talking on the phone with the gardener. She told him she wouldn't need him for a good three months. I knew what that meant. I'd just been assigned some new garden chores as punishment. Then, while I was eating dinner by myself at the kitchen table, I heard my abuela upstairs taking out my game box. And I had a hunch that it wasn't going end there.

As I was finishing up dinner, my abuela came back downstairs. Without saying a word, she rinsed out some cups in the sink. Then she turned around to look me in the eye.

"You boys did the right thing. It's hard to tell the truth, but it's better. Oh my Lord," she said, and then her eyes began to tear up. I got the feeling she was thinking about Vasco and all the wrong turns he'd made in life. She just didn't want me to make the same mistakes.

I knew what she meant about it being better to tell the truth, but that was a hard idea to translate into middle school logic. Ratting was the worst thing you could do, and ratting on your best friends was just about unheard of. I'd just ratted on my best friends, the Conquistadors. I was a certified middle school rat.

That night I stayed up in my room. Back and forth I went from trying to read, to trying to do some homework. My game-box shelf was empty. I couldn't concentrate. My ears were waiting for the sound of the phone ringing. It would be Hernan, or Cisco, or one of the other Conquistadors calling to curse me out for ratting. Nine o'clock passed, then ten, and still nothing. Even Henrietta didn't call. Maybe she'd learned already that I had ratted and didn't want to have anything to do with me. Her pop was a *veterano*, and that was their code. She probably felt the same way. Trying to get it off my mind, I got ready for bed and turned out the lights.

As I lay there, I reasoned that my abuela would understand if I didn't go to school in the morning. She'd want me to stay home after fainting and everything. I could ditch out on school and not think about the whole mess for another day. But when I eventually went again, the mess would all still be there. I'd have to take it all the heat for ratting, all the name-calling, all the dirty looks, and all the shame. It was going to be one hell of a day. Better to get it over with now, I decided. Before I closed my eyes, I prayed.

Chapter 14

SOMEHOW I MANAGED TO HAVE enough courage to get ready for school that morning. I felt like I was just going through the motions. My breakfast cereal had no flavor. And when I left the house, the world looked like a different place to me. It was an odd day to begin with. Gray clouds had been hanging overhead for days. Something felt strange. It was usually sunny this time of year.

Walking to school, I thought about the friendships I'd had since I was a little kid and how they were gone. Before the Conquistadors had started, I'd thought the guys would be my friends forever, that we'd know each other and still goof around when we were my abuela's age. We'd have grandkids, and they'd be like us, friends and all, too. I didn't know anybody in the world as well as I knew those guys. And here I'd ratted on them. It made me feel ashamed just to think about it. Maybe I should've waited another day. Someone else might've ratted by then, and I wouldn't have had to.

Since there was nobody to walk with on my way to school, I went over my plans from the night before. All night long, I had tossed and turned. But finally the answer came to me. I was going to run away. My reputation—or any reputation I thought I had at school and with my friends—was gone. You can't just start over and make new friends in middle school. So it was either leave for good, or stay behind and be known for the rest of my life as Manny the rat.

I'd leave that night. It would be easy for me to pack up a few things and leave in the middle of the night, like I'd done the night we'd gone out to the wash. There was a truck stop down by the freeway. I planned to sneak out of the house and skate down to the truck stop. A lot of folks would sneak in and out of the town at that stop, and I could too, I figured. I'd saved up at least a hundred bucks from the money my parents sent me and from birthdays and stuff. That'd be enough to get me down to Mexico, I was sure. I could find my parents in Guadalajara. I could forget everything that had happened and everything about Orbe Nuevo forever. Sure, I'd miss my abuela, and Bernard and Henrietta, but that's three people against the hundreds of kids at school I'd have to be with every day. There was nothing left for me if I stayed.

One thing that was pulling me to school that morning was curiosity. I had to find out for myself how everything had played out. The kids wouldn't talk to me, I knew, and nobody would want to be seen a hanging around with me. I was Manny the rat of Orbe Nuevo Middle School.

Sure enough, when I got to school, the kids didn't talk to me. The cold shoulders started as soon as I got on the grounds. The Conquistadors weren't in their usual spot at the lunch tables. I guessed they'd been pulled from school by either the cops or the principal. As I walked across the quad, none of the kids said anything to me. Some even turned the other way when they saw me coming. I just focused on making it to my class and tried to ignore everything else.

In class, the cold shoulder treatment continued. Once I sat down, I looked across the room to Henrietta and she immediately turned the other way. It hurt to have her act that way. She had been there with me that night. She was the one who knew we had to do something about the fight. It was her mom, even, who called the cops. We had gone through it all together, and now she was brushing me off. Fine, I thought, glad to know sooner rather than later how'd she'd act. The teacher gave us our work and I started right on it, tuning everything else out.

Second period and third period, went pretty much the same way. There were cold shoulders everywhere. I tried to remember when the school had ever been so quiet, but I couldn't recall a time. It was as if everybody was walking around in a fog, not saying anything, just gliding through the mist.

As fourth period began, I got called to the principal's office. I knew I was in big trouble and expected the worst. When I got to the office, the principal and vice principal were both tied up with other business, so the secretary gave me the news. The authorities had contacted the school, so the faculty and staff were aware of my involvement with the herb, and Carl, and everything. Because of my involvement, I wouldn't be allowed to participate in any extracurricular activities, which included intramural sports. I was also being given clean-up detention three days a week until the end of the school year. Then the secretary told me that further punishment could still be handed out, pending the completion of the investigation. She also told me I only got the deal I got because of my academic success and for being forthright with the authorities. I signed the probation contract, thanked her, and left the office.

I didn't even bother going to the cafeteria for lunch. I went to the library instead, and started reading the Steinbeck book I'd checked out weeks earlier. Soon, I imagined, I'd be just like him, traveling. I'd be on the road seeing new things. When I got to Guadalajara I'd make new friends. I wondered if being a rat was something that people would be able to see on my face, like a certain look in my eyes.

I made it through the school day. There was nobody to walk home with, so I went alone. I noticed Henrietta walking a block ahead of me with some girlfriends. Girls sure can be cold when they want to, I thought. She didn't even turn around to look at me. I also noticed Nicky walking with a couple of other geeks. I thought about jogging up to him and the others, but decided against it. What's the point? You're leaving tonight anyway, I reminded myself.

I started packing as soon as I got home. I wasn't taking a lot, just a couple of pairs of jeans, a couple of shirts, my toothbrush, jacket, and a few books to read. I stuffed them all into my school backpack and put it by the door. I'd throw some sandwiches and drink boxes in there before slipping out later on that night. Thinking that I might not be able to sleep on the road, I was about to take a nap when the phone rang downstairs. Pausing, I listened to my abuela pick it up, and then I heard her footsteps coming up the stairs. It was for me. Not wanting anything to seem unusual, I threw my backpack under my bed and sat down on the floor.

"Manny, it's your girlfriend," my abuela said with a little smile.

Dumbfounded, I didn't know what to do. Henrietta hadn't

said anything to me at school all day, or walked home with me. She'd acted just like the other kids. There's nothing worse than a girlfriend who doesn't hang with you when things aren't going good, I thought. What if she was calling me to curse me out for being a rat? I hesitated.

"Tell her—tell her I'm sick."

"What?" my abuela said, shocked.

I shook my head quickly to signal to my abuela that I didn't want to talk to her. My abuela looked at me curiously, then put the phone in my hand.

"Tell her yourself, Don Juan!" my abuela said with a giggle, then left the room.

I stared at the phone in my hand for a second or two before putting it to my ear. I'd thought I'd never speak to her again. She'd be out of my life forever. I'd be down in Mexico, and she'd be up here. Now what was I supposed to say to her?

"Hello?"

"Did your grandma say you were sick?"

"Kind of. What's up?"

"So what was up with you today?" she asked testily.

"Me?"

"Yeah. You didn't say hi or anything."

"I thought you weren't saying hi to me."

"I wasn't not saying hi to you. You wouldn't even look at me!"

"You weren't looking at *me*! Nobody looked at me. Nobody talked to me," I pleaded.

"Well nobody was talking to anybody, especially after what happened before school."

"What happened before school?"

"You didn't hear?" she asked, like I was stupid or something.

"No. Nobody was talking to me, remember?"

"Oh. Well, those dopey goth girls ratted out your friends. Then your friends started ratting themselves out. Pretty soon everybody was ratting on everybody."

"What? No way!"

"It was so whack. Nicole went to the office before school because she was sick, and she said Ferdinand's parents came in and went into the principal's office. Then she heard the secretary telling an office worker that his parents made Ferdinand tell the truth, or he was going to get whupped right there in the office. His dad didn't care if he got busted for child abuse or not, and was sitting there holding his belt the whole time Ferdinand was talking!"

"No way!"

"Then Nando comes in and sees Ferdindand's parents waiting around, so he goes and tells the same story before his parents even get there, because I guess he figures he's gonna get whupped, too, if he doesn't talk soon enough."

"Are you serious?"

"Then those goth girls get called in, and they start talking about everything, like how Carl was the connect for the gang, and how Hernan and Cisco gave them wine and beer. And your friends are so dumb; they start arguing with the goth girls about how they didn't give them the wine. They only gave them the beer! And with that, they pretty much confessed to everything except giving the goth girls wine!"

I shook my head in disbelief. "What? I don't believe you."

"And that's not all."

"Then what?"

"So security goes and searches everybody's backpacks while they're waiting for parents and cops and people to get there, and they find wine and cigarettes in the goth girls' bags, and pot, speed, and tagging stuff in all your friends' bags."

"Oh no!" I slapped my hand to my forehead.

"Then a call comes from the police station, saying Carl and Victor made a statement and pretty much told the same story, except Carl left out that he was the connect for the Conquistadors, but then he had to admit it when they asked him why he went to the cul de sac in the first place."

"All this happened before school?" I asked.

"Yeah. The cops came and got Hernan and Cisco, like fifteen minutes before first bell. The rest got put on suspension until they figured everything out. By the time you got there, nobody wanted to say anything to anybody, because I guess we all figured somehow we'd get mixed up in it, too."

"Wow." I was astonished. Nobody had been giving me the cold shoulder after all. They were just scared of getting busted.

"I thought everybody was mad at me because, well, yesterday afternoon I told police what happened at the cul de sac. I ratted them out."

"You did?" Henrietta asked, truly shocked.

"Yeah. Are you mad at me?"

Henrietta didn't say anything for a long time. Then she sighed. "Shhh, that's weak."

"So you are mad at me?"

"I don't know. But I'm sure your friends are going to be when they find out."

"I know."

"Well, look at it this way, Manny. It didn't matter in the end, 'cause everybody ratted."

"I guess."

"A couple of my friends asked if you were all right after fainting yesterday, is all. That's the only talk I heard about you, anyway."

I felt like fainting right then and there. It wasn't a stress faint, though; it was more like a relief faint. As she told me the story, everything began to make sense. All the negativity I'd felt at school had been my imagination.

I'd never felt so glad in my life that girls were so gossipy. Hernietta knew everything. Literally floored by it all, I lay down on the carpet after the phone call to let it all sink in. Staring up at the ceiling, I thanked God for helping me avoid being a friendless rat for the rest of my life. I knew at least Henrietta was still talking to me. And even though I still had the Conquistadors to answer to, and my clean-up detention, and the wrath of my abuela to deal with, I felt better knowing that the mess didn't all fall on me. I heard doorbell ring downstairs and wondered who it was on a Wednesday afternoon. Listening hard, I heard what sounded like Bernard, saying hi to my abuela. Then I heard his footsteps racing up the stairs and down the hall to my room. Bernard rushed in holding his skateboard.

"Hey, man! Check this out!" he said excitedly.

He was dripping with water from head to toe.

"What is it?" I asked, not sure yet.

"It's rain. It's raining. We got to roll in this, man. It's awesome!"

"No way," I said, hopping up and running to my window.

I looked outside. The rain was pouring down.

"Come on. Let's roll, man!"

Then suddenly, like she always did when it rained in Orbe Nueuo, I heard my abuela call out from downstairs.

"Manny! Look outside! It's raining! It's raining!"

Writer's Note

When I was younger I tried to write crime fiction and thrillers, which didn't turn out very well. Over the years since then, I became a believer in the Lord and got baptized for the forgiveness of sins and a changing of heart. After having the opportunity to participate in a community-based theater project, I came to learn how stories and the process of writing can help people become better. On my new path, I set out to write those kinds of stories.

DISCARDED